blade silver

color me scarred

melody carlson

DISCARD

7308 1/148

TH1NK Books is an imprint of NavPress. TH1NK is a registered trademark of NavPress. Absence of ® in connection with marks of NavPress or other parties does not indicate an absence of registration of those marks.

ISBN 1-57683-535-9

Cover design by www.studiogearbox.com
Cover photo by Powerstock/Superstock

Creative Team: Nicci Jordan, Arvid Wallen, Erin Healy, Darla Hightower, Pat Reinheimer

This is a work of fiction. The characters, incidents, and dialogues are products of the author's imagination and are not to be construed as real. Any resemblance to actual events or persons, living or dead, is entirely coincidental.

Published in association with the literary agency of Sara A. Fortenberry.

Library of Congress Cataloging-in-Publication Data

Carlson, Melody.
  Blade silver : color me scarred / Melody Carlson.
    p. cm. -- (TrueColors ; bk. 7)
  Summary: Ruth copes with an abusive situation at home by cutting herself, until her high school counselor helps her get the treatment she needs to start a new life.
  ISBN 1-57683-535-9
  [1. Self-mutilation--Fiction. 2. High schools--Fiction. 3. Schools--Fiction. 4. Counselors--Fiction.] I. Title.
  PZ7.C216637Bla 2005
  [Fic]--dc22
                                        2005015748
Printed in the United States of America

3 4 5 6 7 8 9 10 / 09 08 07

Other Books by Melody Carlson

Fool's Gold (NavPress)

Burnt Orange (NavPress)

Pitch Black (NavPress)

Torch Red (NavPress)

Deep Green (NavPress)

Dark Blue (NavPress)

DIARY OF A TEENAGE GIRL series (Multnomah)

DEGREES series (Tyndale)

Crystal Lies (WaterBrook)

Finding Alice (WaterBrook)

Three Days (Baker)

one

SOMETIMES I FEEL LIKE I'M ABOUT TO EXPLODE. OR MAYBE I WILL IMPLODE. I'm not really sure, but I think it's going to get messy. And I think someone's going to get hurt. Probably me.

I turn my CD player up a couple of decibels. Not loud enough to attract his attention—I don't want that—but loud enough to drown out his voice as he rages at my fourteen-year-old brother. I'd like to stand up for Caleb. I even imagine myself going out there and bravely speaking out in my younger brother's defense. But the problem is, I'm just a big chicken.

Besides that, I know what will happen if I try to tell Dad that it's not Caleb's fault, if I try to explain that Mom forgot to give us lunch money again today, and that Caleb was just trying to get by. But I can tell by the volume of Dad's voice that it's already too late for reasoning. And while I can't discern his exact words over the sound of Avril Lavigne's lyrics, I can feel them cutting and slicing through Caleb—and through me.

I imagine my younger brother shredded and bleeding out there. A big red puddle spilled out across the pale yellow linoleum in our kitchen.

My dad never hits us with his fists. He never slaps us around or takes off his belt. He's too concerned about leaving welts or bruises, something that someone might notice. But his words are worse than a beating. And they leave invisible scars—scars that never seem to fade.

Finally it gets quiet out there. I hear Caleb's bedroom door, across the hall from mine, closing quietly. He knows not to slam it. That would only prolong the agony. And after a bit, I hear the door to the garage bang shut and then my dad's Ford diesel truck roaring down the driveway and onto the road.

I know that it's safe to go out now. Still feeling guilty for not defending Caleb, I creep out and stand in the hallway, hovering like a criminal in front of his door, my hand poised to knock softly, ready to go in and tell him I understand how he feels and that I'm sorry, but I can hear him crying now. And I can hear him punching something. It sounds like his pillow or maybe his mattress—*pow pow pow* again and again—and I know that trying to say something to him while he's like this will only make things worse.

The last time I tried to comfort him, he got seriously angry at me. He told me that I didn't understand anything. He said that Dad might come down on me sometimes, but never as hard. "You're Dad's favorite," he finally spat, slamming his door in my face. And so I know better than to say anything when he's feeling this mad. But it worries me. What if he becomes like Dad? What if the day comes when I can't even talk to him about anything?

I look at the closed door at the end of the hallway. My parents' bedroom. I know that Mom is in there. I can hear the little TV playing quietly, strains of that obnoxious *Jeopardy!* theme music. It's her favorite show. When she's feeling good, she can get most of the answers right. But she's been in one of her "down" moods for several weeks now. No telling how long this one will last.

As much as I hate to disturb her when she's like this, I know this is my best chance to ask her for lunch money—for both me and Caleb. Either that or I'll have to see if there's anything in the kitchen that I can use to make us lunches for tomorrow. Either way, I have to make sure that Caleb does not have to borrow money from anyone. I don't know why he went and bummed lunch money from Sally today.

Sally is our cousin. Her family lives in a nicer neighborhood a couple of miles from here, and although she may be good to loan out a buck or two, Caleb should've known she'd tell her dad (who is our dad's older brother). Caleb should've known that Uncle Garrett would call our dad to rib him about Caleb begging money from his precious Sally today. And that's exactly what happened, and that's what ignited our dad's highly volatile fuse tonight.

But in all fairness to Caleb, if it hadn't been the lunch money, it would've been something else. Like a trash can still sitting out on the street, a bike parked in the front yard, shoes left on the floor in the living room . . . it doesn't take much. Dad went ballistic one night last week just because someone left the hose running. Turned out it was him. But he never apologized.

His solution after one of his tirades is to leave here enraged. He goes to one of two places. He wants us to think he's at his friend Jimmy's house, where they mess around with the restoration of an old Corvette and drink cheap beer. But he spends a fair amount of time at The Dark Horse Tavern. It's a sleazy-looking place on one of the side streets downtown. He parks his pickup in the back and hangs out there until he's forgotten whatever it was that made him so angry.

Dysfunctional? Um, *yeah*. But most people looking at our family from the outside are totally clueless. Including Dad's best friend Jimmy and even Uncle Garrett. Despite Uncle Garrett's flaws, I'm sure he has no idea that his younger brother has such an out-of-control anger problem. Most people who know my dad think that he's the "nicest guy in town." He manages Jackson's Tire Company and always has a ready smile or goofy joke for everyone—everyone who doesn't live inside this house, that is. And I'm sure that everyone just looks at our family and assumes everything's just fine and dandy in here. Sure, we might not be impressive when it comes to money, but we are all very adept at keeping up appearances. For some reason that's very important to my dad.

My question is, what am I supposed to do with all this pain? I mean I've got Caleb across the hall now, crying and swearing and pounding on things. I've got my mom holed up in her room, eyes glazed over by Xanax I'm sure, sitting in the little glider rocker next to her bed, just staring at the tiny TV that sits on their bureau. I feel like I'm going to burst.

Instead of returning to my room, I go into the bathroom that Caleb and I share. We do our best not to fight over it like some of my friends do with their siblings—at least not while Dad is around. I sigh as I look into the mirror above the bathroom sink. My face, as usual, is expressionless. Although the eyes would be a giveaway, if anyone was really looking. To me they are two black holes. A constant reminder of the deep hopelessness of my life. I push a strand of straight dark hair out of my face. I've been growing my bangs out, and they've reached that place where they're just in the way. Sort of like me.

It won't be that long, and you can be out of this madhouse for good. Recently I've been playing with the idea of graduating a year early, getting out of here when I'm only seventeen. I've heard it can be done.

The question is, can I really last that long? Every single day I tell myself I'm not going to do this again. I'm not going to give in one more time. And some days I actually succeed. But on other days, like today, it is impossible. The tightness inside my chest is painful right now. And I wonder if a fairly healthy sixteen-year-old can have a heart attack or maybe a stroke. Maybe that would be the answer.

For no particular reason, other than habit, I turn on the tap water and let it just run into the sink. It's how I usually do this thing. Maybe I figure the sound will camouflage what's really going on in here. I don't know. Maybe the swooshing sound relaxes me. Or maybe it's comforting to watch the water flow. Like, there's something that still works. But I just stand there and watch it running down the sink. I don't wash my hands or brush my teeth or wash my face. I simply stand there, hands planted on either side of the sink, as I lean forward and stare at the water flowing from the faucet and going down the drain. I'm sure my dad would think this was not only incredibly stupid but very wasteful. I'm sure if I were ever caught, I would get a sharp-tongued lecture on just how much he pays for the water and electric bill every month and how selfish and ignorant I am. Normally, I do try to be frugal and respectful of his "hard-earned" money, but there are times, like now, when I just don't care.

I don't know how long I stand there wasting valuable water, but finally I turn off the faucet and take a deep breath. I wish I could stop this thing, but I still ache inside. Instead of diminishing, the pain only seems to grow, pushing against my insides until I don't see how I can possibly contain it anymore.

I open the bottom drawer on my side of the bathroom cabinet. It's where I keep my "feminine" products—a place I can be certain that my dad or brother would never go looking. As for my mother, well, she would never think to go looking for anything of mine in the first place. She can hardly find her slippers in the morning.

I take out a box of tampons and turn it over. A sliver of silver glints from where the cardboard overlaps on the bottom. I carefully slide out the blade and hold it between my thumb and forefinger. It's an old-fashioned, two-sided kind of blade. I swiped one from Caleb when he first started shaving with my grandpa's old brass razor set. It didn't take my little brother very long to realize that there are better shaving instruments available, so he never notices when a blade goes missing from the little cardboard box in the back of his drawer. Not that I've had to replace many blades during these past six months. As long as you wash and dry them and keep them in a safe place, they can last quite a while.

At first I thought I would limit my cutting to my left arm. But after a few weeks, I started running out of places to cut. And that's when I realized I'm fairly coordinated when it comes to cutting with my left hand. My right arm has a series of evenly spaced stripes to prove this. I push up the sleeve of my shirt and examine the stripes with regular interest, running my fingers over the ones that are healed, barely touching the ones that are still healing. Each one could tell its own story. Okay, the stories would be pretty similar, but each scar is unique. The most recent cut was only two days ago. It's still pretty sore, but at least it's not infected.

Already I am beginning to feel relief. I have no idea why. But it's always like this. Just the security of holding the blade in my hand, just knowing that I am in control now . . . it's almost enough. But not quite.

I lower the blade to the pale skin on the inside of my arm, and using a sharp corner of the blade, I quickly make a two-inch slash. I know not to go too deep. And when I'm in control, like now, I can do it just right. And just like that, I'm done. I hardly feel the pain of the cut at all. It's like it doesn't even hurt.

I watch with familiar fascination as the blood oozes out in a clean, straight line. There is something reassuring about seeing my bright-red blood exposed like this. It's like this sign that I'm still alive and, weird as it sounds, that someday everything will be okay. Although the euphoria that follows the cutting never lasts as long as I wish it would, it's a quick fix that mostly works.

As usual, I feel better as I press a wad of toilet paper onto the wound. For the moment, this cut absorbs all my attention and emotional energy. It blocks out what I am unable to deal with. And for a while I am convinced that I will actually survive my life.

And, hey, this isn't as bad as doing drugs, like some kids do. Or getting drunk, like my dad is doing right now. Or just checking out, like my mom did last year and continues to do on an off-and-on basis.

Am I proud of my behavior? Of course not. But for the time being, it's all I have to keep me from falling. So don't judge me.

two

I STARTED CUTTING LAST WINTER WHEN EVERYONE WAS WEARING LONG-SLEEVED sweaters and sweatshirts and jackets. It wasn't any big deal to cover up the scars back then. I guess I never thought about what I'd do once the warmer weather came on. I mean, it's not like you plan these things in advance. So here it is, May, and I'm still sporting long-sleeved shirts. Like what choice do I have?

"Aren't you hot in that shirt?" asks my best friend, Abby, as we take our lunches outside to eat in the courtyard. Some of our friends are already gathered on the concrete steps in a sunny southern corner.

"No," I lie. "And don't you get sick of asking me that same question every day?"

"I don't ask that every day."

"Okay. Every other day. But seriously, don't you think I can decide whether I'm hot or not?"

"I think you're hot, Ruth," says Finney with a cheesy grin.

I roll my eyes at him as I sit on the concrete step, balancing my tray on my knees. "Thanks a lot, Finney," I say in my best sarcastic tone. Now, most people think of Finney as a total nerd. And I guess he sort of is with his bad haircut and wire-rimmed glasses. He's also pretty scrawny and actually uses a plastic pocket protector and multicolored highlighter pens, which he uses for specific reasons that only Finney understands. A stranger might even assume that he's retarded or, to be more PC, "mentally challenged." But he's not. He just looks like he doesn't have much going on. Except brains. That and a slightly whacked-out sense of humor.

"No problem," he shoots back at me. "And like I said last week, Ruth, I'd still love to take you to the prom. I'd be proud to be your man, babe."

I exhale loudly, showing exasperation. "And like I told you last week, Finney, I'd still rather be stripped naked and tied down to an anthill."

"And like I told you," he winks at me, "I'm up for that option too."

Everyone laughs and Abby changes the subject. I listen kind of absently, watching as my friends so easily interact with each other. Sometimes, like right now, it feels like I'm not really here. I suppose it was Abby's comment on my long-sleeved shirt that set me apart, reminded me of my difference. Times like this make me feel like I'm on the outside looking in. Or maybe invisible.

I have to admit, at least to myself, that I am hot—not *hot* as in good-looking, but as in, I think it's nearly ninety degrees out here in the direct sun. Everyone else has on T-shirts and tank tops and even shorts. But here I sit, wearing what's become my uniform: a long-sleeved shirt with sleeves that nearly cover my hands, tan corduroy overalls with a hole in the left knee, and my old Doc Martens sandals that I've had for like a hundred years now. My dark hair is crookedly parted in the middle and braided into two long braids that reach nearly to my waist. I used to hate it back in grade school when Mom put my hair into what other kids called "pigtails." I was already well aware of her Native American heritage—but I didn't feel the need to go around advertising it. And whenever I wore braids, Brett Hamlin would tease me. He'd pull on a tail and call me "injun" or "squaw girl" or "red face," and I didn't really appreciate the attention.

I scoot over to catch some shade and perhaps blend into the wall. I do feel a little self-conscious about my lack of style today. It's not like I think this is my best look. But it's all I'm able to manage on some days. Like today. Thankfully, my friends haven't boycotted my friendship based on my appearance yet.

I mean, it's not exactly like I hang with the fashionable crowd anyway. You need lots of money and even more superficiality to do that. No, I prefer to hang with what I like to consider the "artsy" group. We are involved in drama, art, journalism, or something else that loosely qualifies as artsy. Or else, like Abby, who is challenged to draw a circle, we're connected to someone who is artsy. In her case that would be me.

I'm pretty much into art and journalism. And, according to Mrs. Napier, my graphic-design teacher, I may have some talent, perhaps even "a future." Of course, when I mentioned this at home, my dad said there is no future in art. Just like that—case closed. Naturally, I didn't argue with him. I mean, it's not like I need to go around looking for disagreements with him.

"How about you, Ruth? Are you ready?"

I look up to see that it's this new guy, Glen Something-or-Other, talking to me now. I'm sure my face looks totally blank. "Huh?" I say, adding more dumbness to the increasingly pathetic image.

"Earth to Ruth," teases Abby as she gives me an elbow.

"The art fair tomorrow night," explains Glen. "Have you got your stuff all matted and framed yet?"

I shake my head. "No, I'll probably have to stay after school and finish it up today."

"Me too," he says. "Maybe you can help show me where stuff is in the art room."

"You have some pieces to show?" I can't hide my surprise. "I mean, you just started school here last week."

"Mr. Pollinni said I can show some of the things I was working on before I transferred."

"Cool," I tell him. "That seems only fair." Of course, I don't admit to him or anyone else that this news concerns me quite a bit. I mean, I don't like to sound conceited, but I thought I had a pretty good chance of getting a prize or two for my own pieces. I even hoped that maybe my parents would show up and be impressed when they saw a blue ribbon hanging from one of my acrylics. It could happen.

Now I'm not so sure. I mean, even though Glen's only been here a week, I've already noticed him working on a great-looking sketch. I could tell right away that this guy is really talented. Probably way more talented than me.

"I gotta go," I say as I rise to my shabbily shod feet.

"But there's still a few minutes," says Abby.

"I know," I say. "But I just remembered I need to make a phone call."

"A phone call?" She looks skeptical. "Who to? And, anyway, just use my cell, Ruth. That is, if I can find it in here." She's rooting around in her oversized bag now.

"That's okay," I say as I start to leave. "I'm in a hurry. See ya."

I know that Abby can see right through my stupid little lie. I mean seriously, a *phone call*? How lame is that? But it's like I just need to get away. First of all, I was cooking in that sun. Then the news about Glen getting to show his art from his old school. No telling how good it is, or if it's even from this year like it's supposed to be. He could show up with all kinds of stuff that could really make me look bad. I can't take this.

I go into the bathroom and then into the farthest stall from the entrance, where I close and lock the metal door. I tell myself to just breathe and relax—I heard this bit of advice on one of those late-night radio-shrink shows. Like anyone would need someone to tell them to breathe, although in my case it might be true. But as I'm slowly breathing in and out, I start to think I'm hyperventilating and get worried that I might pass out, crash into the door, get a concussion, and end up looking like the school idiot as I'm carried out of here on a stretcher.

Okay, I totally hate cutting at school. It's not only stupid but risky. Like what if someone saw me or figured this out? I've heard some of my friends talking about cutters in the past. Lish Mackey almost bled to death on the baseball field last fall when she cut too deeply once. Abby thought it was "totally freaky." Others said things like, "I just don't get it," or "That is so lame," or "Why would anyone want to inflict pain on herself?" or "It must just be a pathetic cry for attention." Maybe I'm the one who actually said that last thing.

And so when I first began doing this, I swore I would never, never do this at school. And, really, why would I? I mean, the stuff with my dad was mainly what pushed me over the edge. In fact, I used to consider school to be a fairly safe place. I have my friends, my art, my classes . . . For the most part, I actually like being here. Not that I'd ever admit that to anyone.

Still, things happen. Like some rude chick will make some stupid comment about my race or my clothes or whatever, and suddenly I'm feeling uptight. Or something goes wrong in a class, like I get offended by some thoughtless teacher. It happens. But because of those unpredictable little scenarios, I eventually broke my promise to myself and took action. I'm always prepared now. I do what I've got to do to get by, whatever it takes to give me back some control, to help me cope.

With shaking hands, I hang my backpack on the hook on the door, unzip the small pocket on the outside, and pull out what appears to be an innocent box of Altoids. While there are a few "curiously strong" peppermints in there for effect, under that piece of powdery paper is an even more curiously strong item. I've taped a razor blade securely to the bottom of the tin. I carefully remove it.

I came up with this little plan when I realized that a razor blade might show up on the metal detectors that we walk through at the front doors every morning. Although everyone says they don't really work and are only there to scare us, I wasn't so sure. So I figured no one would suspect anything from an innocent tin of Altoids. And so far, no one has.

I think this is only about my fourth or maybe fifth time to cut at school. And already I have a system. I sit on the toilet, roll up my sleeve, get a giant wad of toilet paper all ready, and then I slice. There's no room for mistakes here. I can't sneak into my room and change my blood-spattered clothes, and the cut can't be so deep that it will bleed for very long. Also, I am equipped with bandages. Plenty of bandages.

I take a deep breath—actually asking myself if I really need to do this—but then I imagine Glen's smug face as he collects every prize and ribbon at the art fair. And then I cut.

Like a drug, that warm feeling rises up in me, a sense that I have control again, that everything's going to be just fine. Then I watch the red ribbon of blood for just a split second before I press the toilet paper onto it. I breathe deeply, and for the moment I am fine. Perfectly fine.

I hear girls coming and going . . . using sinks, toilets, mirrors. Fixing their faces and chatting about things that don't really matter. And finally it's quiet and I hear a bell ringing outside and know that I'm going to be late if I don't hurry. I put a large bandage over my cut, pleased with how perfectly it covers the wound. Then I pull my sleeve down, carefully replace the razor blade in the Altoids box, return this to my pack, and emerge from the stall as if nothing abnormal just happened in there.

I feel a mixture of pleasure and relief as I walk to geometry class, slipping into a rear seat just before the bell rings. But these feelings are laced with guilt. It seems I can never completely escape the realization that this is wrong. And there's fear too—a constant nagging dread that someone may suspect me. Someone may know what I've been doing. Worse, what would happen if that someone told my dad?

three

"DID YOU MAKE YOUR PHONE CALL?" ABBY ASKS ME AFTER GEOMETRY.

"Yeah." I glance away, pretending to study a flyer that's plastered on a post. It's about an HIV-awareness meeting next week. Like I'm really interested.

"Why didn't you just use my cell?" she persists as we walk down the hallway.

"I don't know." Now, I don't like to lie to my best friend, but cutting is my one exception. It's like it falls into this special clause in "the one and only thing you don't have to tell your best friend" section. So I continue my charade. "It was about my mom," I say in a serious voice.

"Oh?" I can tell this gets her attention and, I'm sure, her concern too. "Is everything okay?"

Abby knows a lot about my family. Probably more than anyone, including our extended family of aunts, uncles, and grandparents. And she knows that my mom pretty much had a nervous break-down last winter. Oh, we don't call it that. We call it "When Mom Got Sick," like it's the title of a bad movie or something. But Mom got more than just sick. She went flipping crazy. Just a week before Christmas, she ran away from home and checked into a really expensive hotel, where she took an overdose of sleeping pills and nearly killed herself. Actually, that was her goal—to kill herself. But no one talks about *that*. Even Abby is unaware of that particular scene. After Mom was discovered by a maid, she spent some time in the kind of hospital where mental patients are taken in for evaluation and treatment.

I'm not sure what the evaluation was, but treatment involved some pretty heavy doses of things like Xanax to calm her down and Prozac to wake her up. Now she takes a "cocktail" of these little pills every day. Rather, my dad doles out her daily portion of drugs then locks up the prescription bottles in his gun safe. But sometimes, like if she's not up yet, he leaves them with a glass of water by her bed. And then she sometimes "forgets" to take them. That's when things get messier than usual.

"Yeah, it's pretty much okay now," I tell Abby. "But Mom forgot to take her Prozac yesterday, and that sort of messed her up, you know. So I promised to call her at lunch today—to make sure she didn't forget again."

"Your poor mom." Abby shakes her head. "She's been through so much this year."

"You're telling me." I feel a wave a relief. Not only does my story get me off the hook, it's garnered some genuine sympathy too. Besides, in some ways it's not completely untrue. Mom did forget to take her meds yesterday. And maybe I should call her to remind her today. But chances are I'd only wake her up, and I always feel so bad to have disturbed her during the day. Sometimes I think the only time she really rests is when no one is home. I often hear her walking around the house at night. Sometimes she cleans things. Sometimes she just sits in the living room with the lights off and does nothing. It's kind of like having a ghost mom in the house.

"Well, maybe you should have a special code for something like that," Abby says just as we're about to part ways for our next class.

"Huh?"

"You know, like when you need to call and check on your mom. Like maybe you could say that you've got to go to the bathroom."

"Yeah, right. I'm gonna do that."

"Well, something."

"How about I say I have to go make a phone call?"

Abby kind of smiles. "Yeah, whatever."

Then before I can go she grabs my arm—the same arm I just cut—and I wince. "What's wrong?" she asks.

"Nothing." I fake a smile. "Just pulled a muscle in my calf during PE today. It still kinda hurts."

"Yeah, well, I don't want to forget. I have something to tell you. Something important!"

"Okay, but hurry, I want to get to art."

"Yeah, but you need to hear this first."

"What?" I feel my impatience growing.

"Glen Collins," she says with the kind of urgency that should be self-explanatory but unfortunately is not.

"Yeah?" I say without revealing any real interest, but I'm thinking, *So that's his last name. Collins.* "What about him?"

"I think he likes you."

I roll my eyes. "Right. Tell me another one."

"Seriously, Ruth. He asked about you after you left. And the way he asked questions makes me think he's really interested. Even poor Finney was acting a little worried."

I kind of laugh. "Like Finney has something to worry about."

"Well, I honestly think Glen likes you. And I just thought you should be forewarned."

"Forewarned?" I study her. "Like for what?"

She shrugs. "I don't know. Put your best foot forward."

I actually laugh now. Then I stick out my right foot, showing off my beat-up old sandal. "Would that be this one?"

"I don't know, Ruth. But I happen to think he's a pretty cool guy. And, hey, if you're not interested, leave him for some of us who are."

I peer at her. "Meaning you're into him?"

"I could be. But not if you are. Can't you see that I'm the one who's standing here telling you that I think he's into you? Don't you get it?"

I smile and thank her, then take off running toward art. Not that I think Mr. Pollinni would actually mark me late. He hardly checks to see who's there or not anyway, and I am, after all, one of his favorites. That is, until Glen came along. Now I can't be too sure. And it probably doesn't help matters knowing that Mr. Pollinni is gay. Okay, this is a big secret. I mean, lots of people suspect as much, but I happen to know for a fact since I've met one of his boyfriends (a decorator from San Francisco—talk about obvious!). But anyway, Glen is a good-looking guy, and very artistic. What if he now captures Mr. Pollinni's attention and favor? I have to be careful.

I gently touch my arm, checking my bandage beneath my sleeve. Abby really grabbed it hard and it's throbbing now. I sigh as I hurry into the classroom and wonder if everyone's life is as complicated as mine. I notice Glen in the back of the room. He's laying a big black portfolio on a table. I'm guessing it's filled with all his amazing art from his former school. I envision him pulling out pieces reminiscent of Van Gogh or Picasso or maybe even Andy Warhol.

And then he looks up, his eyes meet mine, and I remember what Abby just told me. Oh, I know she's nuts and just getting carried away in over-the-top Abby fashion. But somehow when he smiles,

I'm not so sure. Anyway, I smile back and then I feel my cheeks growing warm. I'm embarrassed! Why should I be embarrassed? So I just turn away, go to my regular spot at a middle table, drop my backpack onto the dusty floor, and then head to my art locker.

I go on like this, as if nothing whatsoever is out of the ordinary. I get my current project (a pen-and-ink drawing of an old gas station) and get my supplies and go back to my table. Oh, I'm not a zombie. I say "hey" to my art buddies. I look at Kelsey's acrylic of her two cats (a little docile for my taste), and I tell her it's "very nice" then go back to my seat and become absorbed in my work.

Now here's the challenge with pen-and-ink drawings—charcoal can be even worse—but if you're wearing long sleeves you have to be really careful not to let the edge of your sleeve drag over what you've just done. And I can't roll up my sleeves. So what I've done is made these little holes that I slip my thumbs into, which hold my sleeves fairly taut. It helps some, but I still have to watch it or I'll ruin all my hard work.

"Looking good, Ruth," says Glen from behind me.

I don't look up but just nod. "Thanks."

"Do you think it'll be done in time for the art fair tomorrow night?"

I shrug. "I don't know. It's close. Maybe I'll take it home to finish tonight." Even as I say this, I know for a fact that I won't. I hate taking any art project home. Not that I don't like doing art in the privacy of my room. I do. But I just don't like taking the chance of being seen by my dad carrying something through the house that he might ask about. Besides that, he has absolutely no problem snooping around in my room, and chances are he would find my project.

When that happens, one of two things usually results: (1) He makes some dismissive remark about how art is a waste of time in public school and how taxpayers' money should be put to better use, like sports programs, or (2) he makes a comment about the actual work or the subject matter. He never approves of what I choose to draw or paint. "Why do you like such dark and depressing things?" he'll ask me. "No wonder you're such a gloomy girl. Why don't you paint something cheerful for a change?"

So I don't take my artwork home. And even when it comes to the sketch pad in my room, which I rarely use, I always make sure to keep it safely out of sight, usually under my mattress. Not that I think my dad won't look there, but I just try to keep it out of sight if he's around. It's just not worth the fuss.

"Do you usually ride the bus home?"

I turn around and look at him now. "Huh?"

"You know, after school. Do you ride the bus?"

I make a face. "Not if I can help it."

"You have a car?"

"No. I bum rides off Abby."

"But I thought I saw you getting on the bus yesterday."

I consider this. Like what is he, some kind of stalker or something? "Yeah," I admit. "I had to take the activities bus yesterday since I stayed late to work on the yearbook."

"You're on the yearbook?"

I nod and return to my work. I really do want to get this done in time for the art fair. Now I'm wondering if he's sabotaging me. Is he purposely trying to slow me down so that his chances will be even better?

"I was on yearbook staff at my old school."

I glance back up at him. And I am surprised to see that his expression looks a little sad and slightly lost. And this gets to me. I set my ink pen down on the paper towel and turn my attention fully to him. "Was it hard switching schools like that? I mean so close to the end of the year?"

He nods. "Yeah. But there wasn't much I could do about it."

"Sorry."

Now he brightens some. "Anyway, what I was getting to was that maybe I could give you a ride home tonight. I mean, since we're both staying late to work on matting and stuff."

I nod then turn back to my drawing. "Sure," I tell him. "That'd be great. Way better than the smelly activities bus."

"Okay then . . . " he exhales loudly. "Guess I better let you get back to your work."

And I do. But even as I do, I am wondering, *Maybe Abby is right. Maybe he does like me.* And suddenly I want to turn around and really check this guy out more carefully. I mean, so far I haven't really given him the time of day. And now I'm wondering why.

After about ten minutes, I come up with the need to exchange my dark inky water for something a bit clearer (which I normally don't do often enough). I walk back to the sink, past where Glen is sitting, now intently working on his pencil sketch, and I carefully look him over from my position by the sink.

"What're you staring at?" asks Kelsey as she reaches past me to get some paper towels.

"Nothing," I say quickly. "Just spacing, I guess."

She gives me a look that says she's not convinced. Then she glances over to where I was staring, right where Glen is still sitting hunched over his drawing. "Yeah, you and me both," she finally says. "I'm feeling a little spacey myself." Then she laughs.

I make my face blank, as if I have absolutely no idea what she's talking about, then go back to my table and immerse myself in getting the lettering right on the crooked sign that's hanging over the old gas station. But what I'm seeing in my mind's eye is Glen Collins.

I'm guessing he's a little taller than six feet and medium weight. His hair is that kind of sandy brown color that gets lighter during the summer. And his eyes are this clear shade of blue. But his profile might just knock my socks off. He's got the straightest nose, a very determined mouth, and a strong chin with just the slightest cleft. All in all, this guy is not a bit hard on the eyes. Funny I hadn't noticed earlier. I mean, he's not flashy. Not like, say, Byron Nash—the "heartthrob of Sumner High." But then Byron's not really my type. Too perfect. Besides, I'm sure he gets his teeth whitened, and I think that's so phony. But the fact is that most of the girls in this school are ga-ga over him. And in Byron's defense, he's actually a pretty nice guy.

Suddenly I am hearing Kelsey talking rather loudly in the back of the room. By the tone of her voice, I'd say she is trying to sweet-talk someone. I wonder if she's working over poor Mr. Pollinni, trying to get him to compliment her kitty-cat picture. But when I turn to see, I realize that she's doting on Glen, lathering on praise for his current piece of artwork.

To my disappointment, he seems to be enjoying the attention. But then who doesn't appreciate being admired from time to time, even if by someone who thinks Elvis on velvet is a form of artwork?

But I feel irritated too. It's not that I have anything against Kelsey personally. And I even encouraged her to stick with art, not because I thought she had any talent, but because I thought it would help her grow as a person. See, Kelsey is part of the "popular" crowd. Not that I care about that. But I suppose I sometimes envy those kids, since they seem to have it so easy.

It's like they go around running the school with their smiles and charm and witty remarks. Sometimes I honestly believe that their biggest problems are things like "What should I wear today? Gucci or Prada?" I mean, their skin, hair, teeth, clothes . . . They all look like what you see in fashion magazines or on TV shows like *The OC* or *Laguna Beach*. And while my friends and I tell each other that these kids are spoiled rotten and pretty superficial, I'm sure we all experience a little jealousy from time to time—not that we would ever admit to it. I certainly wouldn't.

So as I sit here, watching Kelsey leaning over Glen's table, her thick blonde hair cascading like it belonged in a Pantene commercial, hearing her lightly amused laughter and her quirky compliments, I feel not only jealous but totally hopeless as well. Because, as I quickly reassess Glen Collins, I realize that he looks like one of them too. With Kelsey's attention, it's only a matter of time before he gets pulled straight into her crowd. It figures.

To make matters worse, when I come back to earth and look down at my own table and artwork, I notice that my left thumbhole has come loose and my ugly wrist with red welts and nasty scars is in full view for all to see. I tug the sleeve back down, glancing around to make sure that no one has witnessed this. But my heart is racing with fear, and I realize that my fleeting fantasy of getting involved with someone like Glen Collins was nothing more than that—a fantasy. Well, that mixed up with a bit of temporary insanity. What was I thinking?

four

MY LAST CLASS IS OVER, AND I HURRY BACK TO THE ART ROOM TO WORK ON matting my art. I'm not sure whether I expect Glen to be there or not. But I'm telling myself I don't care. Why should I care? I mean why would someone like Glen be interested in someone like me—someone whose life is so messed up that she mutilates herself? What do I think—that Glen can't wait to go out with a girl whose arms resemble Frankenstein's?

I mean, summer is here. How can I go around hiding my arms when all my friends are wearing tank tops, sundresses, swimsuits? What kind of freak goes around wearing long-sleeved shirts year-round?

"Hey, Ruth," calls a voice from behind me.

"Glen." I try to be casual, as if I wasn't just obsessing over the fact that I don't have a chance with this guy. "How's it going?"

"Okay."

"I mean, are you feeling a little more at home here?"

"I guess it's going okay," he tells me as we go into the art room. "I'm actually kind of looking forward to this art fair."

"I'll bet you are," I say in a teasing voice. "I can hardly wait to see what's in that portfolio. I'll bet you're going to win all the awards."

"Oh, I doubt it." Then he pauses and looks at me. "Are you

worried, Ruth? I mean I realize you're probably one of the most talented artists at Sumner. You don't think I'm competition, do you?"

Now I'm fairly embarrassed. Does this guy read minds or what? "I don't know." Then I figure, why not just be honest? "Okay, I guess I'm a little concerned. I mean, you show up here out of nowhere and I've seen the drawing you're working on. It's really good, Glen. I wouldn't be surprised if you totally clean up at the art fair. And, hey, you've got every right to—"

"Don't be so sure, Ruth. I've seen your work too, and I'm totally impressed. I think you're way more talented than I—"

"Okay, okay . . . " I hold up my hands as in surrender. "Maybe we should just get this over with. I want to see what's in that portfolio and I want to see it now."

Glen just laughs then takes me by the shoulders (thankfully not the arms) and gently pushes me to the back of the room. "Okay, Ruth. You asked for it." He plants me in front of a table then goes to get his stuff.

I feel slightly breathless as I wait for him to open his portfolio, but I can't say whether that's due to anticipation or how good it felt when he touched me on the shoulders just now. But I stand in silence, imagining a drumroll, as he pulls out one piece after the next. And, here's what's weird, his art reminds me an awful lot of my own.

"Wow," I finally say, then sigh deeply.

"Relieved?"

"No, no . . . that's not it. I still think you're good. Really good."

"What then?"

"Well . . . " I look up at his face, wondering if he has noticed what I'm noticing. "Have you seen very many of my pieces yet?"

"Just a few. Like the one you're working on, the two on the wall. I know Mr. Pollinni thinks you're pretty hot stuff."

I kind of smile. "Well, let me show you some more."

I go to my locker and remove my own portfolio. I lay it on a nearby table and slowly open it. Now I have to admit that I never enjoy showing my work to anyone besides Mr. Pollinni, and sometimes Abby. Most people don't totally get it. And some people, like my dad, think it's depressing. But art's just like that for me. It's like it mirrors my life. If people can't respect that, then how can they respect me?

I start removing the pieces, laying them off to the side, pausing for a few seconds, then removing another and laying it on top of the last one. On I go, waiting for Glen to say something— anything—but he is just staring. Finally I lay the last piece on top. It's one of the last charcoals I did before I started cutting and found my long sleeves made things messy because they smeared the charcoal. The drawing is of a twisted old oak tree that's been hit by lightning and is still smoldering.

"Very cool," says Glen in a voice that sounds almost reverent.

"Seriously?"

He nods. "It feels very familiar, Ruth."

I look into his eyes. "I know."

"They say a picture's worth a thousand words," he says. "But I think we need to talk."

So we work together, picking out mat-board colors, cutting mats, helping each other to make our work look as good as possible, talking the whole while. Talking and talking and talking. And I am amazed by what we have in common. Mostly in the area of dads, although to my amazement, his dad sounds way worse.

"My mom finally got a restraining order on my dad," he tells me as he holds up a matted piece for my approval.

I nod. "That's perfect."

"But he still kept coming around. Finally my mom was really scared. She thought he might kill her before the police took the whole thing seriously."

"That's so wrong."

"I know. So she just pulled out a map and picked a place, and my grandma gave us enough money to move here." He glances over his shoulder now. "Don't tell anyone, but Collins isn't even our real name."

"Really?"

He nods as he slices a nice crisp edge into the black mat board. I can't help but stare at the blade of the mat cutter. It looks so sharp and efficient. I randomly wonder how it would feel against my skin. "Yeah. I probably shouldn't tell you my real name," he's saying. "Not that you'd tell, but—"

"No," I say quickly. "Don't tell me. I mean I totally understand. And, trust me, I won't repeat any of this to anyone."

"Yeah, me too. Not that your family is nearly as twisted as mine."

"At least your dad doesn't live with you anymore."

"Yeah, that's worth something." He turns the mat to cut the other side. "Why do your parents stay together?"

I haven't told him much about my mom yet. I'm not even sure where to begin. Plus, his mom sounds pretty cool. She has a job and a life and the confidence to stand up to her husband. "My mom is, uh . . . well, she's Native American." I wait for his reaction.

"Cool," he says. "So that's where you get those great eyes and that hair."

I feel a warm rush and hope that my cheeks aren't flushed. "Well, my mom's had a hard time with my dad. I mean, he never hits her or us, but my mom has been pretty well beat-up by his words after all these years. She kind of cracked up last winter."

His brow creases in concern. "Man, that must be tough, Ruth."

His sympathy only causes a large lump to grow in my throat. "Yeah, it can get pretty depressing."

"Good that you have your art." He overlays the mat on one of my drawings. "It's a good outlet for pain."

I nod. "Yeah, I guess. But my dad thinks I should do happier subjects."

Glen kind of laughs. "Well, tell your dad he should do the same."

"Yeah, right."

Finally I have to redirect the conversation. All this focus on family is making me feel stressed. I mean, I'm glad that Glen understands. But his life has settled down. He's finally experiencing some relief and stability. I'm happy for him and everything, but my life is still pretty much a mess. And, well, there's the whole cutting thing. No way am I going to tell him about that.

It's almost six, and even though I already phoned home to leave a message about where I am and what I'm doing, I know it's time to get going. "Do you mind if we quit now?" I ask.

He glances up at the clock. "Sure. I had no idea it was so late. I'll bet we can finish up these last few tomorrow."

So we put stuff away, turn out the lights, and head out to the parking lot. I am surprised at how nice Glen's car is. Somehow after hearing the story of the abusive dad, I imagined that he and his mom would be strapped. But here he is, driving a fairly new Honda Accord.

"Nice car," I tell him as I get in.

"Thanks." He starts the ignition. "My mom tried to talk me into trading it for something else—because my dad got it for me on my sixteenth birthday—but I was already kind of used to it. Besides, I think this has to be one of the most common cars in the country. I can't imagine my dad tracking us down based on the make of my car."

"You wouldn't think so."

"Yeah. My dad got me this car as kind of a payoff after he beat me up one night. No broken bones, but my mom took photos, and not long after that came the restraining order. But I refused to press charges."

"Why?"

He shrugs. "I don't know. It just didn't seem right. I mean, he's my dad. And then, of course, he got me the car, and . . . well, I didn't know what to do."

"Yeah, it gets pretty complicated."

I give him directions to my house. "It's not a very impressive neighborhood," I tell him. I don't know why I even care, but after seeing his car, I'm guessing that he and his mom might live in a fairly nice house. And my friend Abby and most of my relatives live in better neighborhoods. So I guess insecurity just comes with the territory.

Not that we live in the slums or the projects. It's not that bad. And, as my dad will point out to any of us, at least we own our house. He'll also point out that he works hard managing the tire store, and that "unlike some of your mom's low-life relatives who live off of the government, I pay my own way. I put food on the table and a roof over your heads!" How many times have I heard that little speech?

But as Glen pulls his car into the asphalt driveway of our yellow ranch-style house with three bedrooms and two baths, I still feel embarrassed. "Well, this is it," I say unceremoniously. "Thanks for the lift."

"No problem. And thanks for the help with the matting today." He smiles a totally endearing smile. "And thanks for listening. It is totally cool to meet someone who really gets me."

I nod and smile. "Yeah."

"See you tomorrow."

I close the car door and walk slowly toward my house. I'm hoping that Glen will drive away before I make it to the door. I don't want to risk having my dad make a sudden appearance and doing something that will thoroughly embarrass me. Thankfully, I make it quietly into the house.

But that's where the quiet ends.

five

"Where have you been?" my dad demands when I'm barely through the front door.

"I told you this morning that I planned to stay late after school. And I left a phone message."

"Why did you have to stay late?" He blocks my way to the kitchen. "Were you in trouble?"

"I was working in the art room. Getting things ready for the art fair tomorrow." Although I'm exasperated, I try to keep my voice even. I don't want to be accused of "sassing" him.

"Who brought you home?"

I look down at the floor and consider lying and saying it was Abby, and that she was using someone else's car, but this whole thing could get blown totally out of proportion if he figures it out. "Glen."

"Glen? *Glen WHO?* I don't know anyone named *Glen.*"

"Glen Collins. He's a new kid at school. He was getting some of his stuff ready for the show too. He offered me a ride."

"A *new* kid in school? So you hardly know this kid and you let him drive you home?"

"He seems nice and responsible. And his car was nice."

"So you think that just because someone has a nice car means that he's a nice person? Ruth Anne Wallace, don't be so naive! Next thing you know you'll be riding off with some serial killer, saying, '*He seemed so nice.*'"

"Sorry." I glance into the kitchen. "Want me to start some dinner?" I offer in the hope that my interrogation is over.

"Where's your brother?"

I look up, slightly worried. Caleb is usually home by now. "I don't know. Isn't he here?"

"If he was here, would I be asking you where he is?" My dad swears. Not a really bad word, but it's a sure sign that he's losing it. "You kids are so selfish. You think you can just take off and run around, doing your own thing, without a thought or concern for anyone else who lives in this house." He usually starts moving around once he starts to rant. As a result, I'm able to slip past him into the kitchen.

"Sorry, Dad," I say, hoping I sound more sincere than I am, "but I haven't seen Caleb since this morning."

My dad stops and scowls at me. Then he moves closer and looks at me with a distrustful expression. "And you *really* don't know where he is, Ruth?"

I shake my head.

"I can hear your brains rattling, Ruth. Are you saying you don't know where your brother is? Or are you just trying to cover for him?"

"I really don't know. Maybe you should call Andy's house."

"I told him to stay away from Andy just last week. I saw that kid hanging outside of the 7-Eleven, and he was smoking."

Of course, I don't reveal that Caleb smokes too. I've warned him that Dad will totally freak if he ever catches on. But I guess smoking is just Caleb's small way of rebelling. My dad launches into a lecture on how stupid it is for teens to start smoking. On and on he goes, like he thinks someone is listening.

Just as he's getting onto tobacco companies and how they're plotting to take over the world, my unfortunate brother comes home. And, man, does that set off a whole new bunch of fireworks. Dad switches subjects midsentence, lashing into Caleb about responsibility and maturity and how Caleb is such a "sorry excuse of a son." Regular stuff like that.

The weird thing is that Caleb's acting like he doesn't even care. And he's got this strange look in his eyes. Like he's up to something or has some kind of an escape plan. I don't know, but I can tell something's up with him. Something's different.

There's nothing I can do to help Caleb. Who knows, maybe he doesn't need any help. So I slink off to my room. But as I go, I notice the door to my parents' bedroom is open a few inches, like maybe she's been standing there listening to this whole thing. Then the door silently closes. I don't even hear the latch click.

I imagine my mom standing behind it, probably still in her faded green bathrobe, her graying hair drooping around her dull eyes. The face that I used to think was pretty is probably just expressionless now. Maybe she's clutching that ugly old afghan, wrapping it around her despite the warmth of the afternoon.

And suddenly I'm furious. Why does she have to be like this? Why can't she say something? Do something? Stand up for her children? Sometimes I really, really hate that woman.

Okay, I know that's not fair. And, really, I do love my mom and I do feel sorry for her, but sometimes her weakness totally disgusts me. I've heard that you dislike the same thing about others that you can't stand in yourself. Maybe that's my problem. Maybe I'm just like her. I mean, it's not like I'm standing up for my brother, either. But like I said, he doesn't seem to need me tonight. Somehow I think he's getting the upper hand. But how? What's he doing differently? Maybe he's just learned not to care. I plan to ask him. Later, when things cool down. Maybe I'll make him a sandwich and go into his room and we can have a real talk.

I hear a loud *smack*, like the sound of a piece of wood breaking, and the chaos of our lives takes on a whole new twist. I hear Caleb yelling and cussing. I run out to see what's going on, and from the hallway I can see that Caleb's nose is bleeding. He looks both shocked and furious.

"Don't you *ever* use that kind of language around me again!" my dad yells. I peek a bit farther around the corner until I can see my dad. And I can tell that he is shocked too. I mean, he never hits us. At least not until now.

"You're evil!" Caleb yells at my dad. "Totally evil. And I'm not taking it anymore." Then Caleb turns and walks right out the front door. Just like that. I mean he's only fourteen. Where's he going? And what's he going to do? And what will happen when he wants to come back? Poor Caleb.

I quietly retreat to my room, thankful that Dad didn't see me watching. I can hear him storming around in the kitchen, probably fixing himself something to eat. And after about twenty minutes he is gone.

First I pace in my bedroom. So far, despite all the stress I'm feeling, I have somehow resisted the urge to cut myself. Maybe getting to know Glen, hearing a story that's similar to mine, has given me this speck of hope. Maybe that's what makes me want to handle my life differently. To quit cutting.

Or maybe the shock of my dad crossing that line is what holds me back. I still can't believe he actually hit Caleb. Hit him hard, it looked like. What happens after this? Where do we go from here?

I can't take it anymore. I march down the hallway and knock on my mom's door. Someone has to start being the grown-up in this house.

After what seems to be a very long time, the door finally opens about six inches wide, and I can see her thin face peering at me. "What?" Her voice is small, like it's from a child who's been punished.

"We need to talk," I say, pushing open the door. I walk right in. I'm not even sure why I feel so bold. I usually avoid going into this room at all. And I can tell she's surprised, but she says nothing, just sits in her glider, sinking down as if it's a struggle to stand.

"Mom," I begin in a pleading voice, almost like I used to talk to her before she had her breakdown. "This is all wrong. I can't stand the way we live. I mean, Dad actually hit Caleb tonight. Did you know that? Caleb's nose was actually bleeding. And then Caleb took off. And who can blame him? I don't even know where he went, or if he's coming back." I pause and just look at my mom, and her face is so blank that you'd think the woman was deaf and dumb. "Can you hear a single word I'm saying?" I demand loudly, disrespectfully. I'm afraid I sound just like my dad.

Her eyes dart to the door, fearful, as if she can hear Dad in my voice too. But still she says nothing. Just sits there. Good grief, this woman can't even help herself. How can I expect her to help Caleb or me?

"Fine." I turn around in anger. "Whatever!"

According to the little digital clock that I put in the bathroom to keep Caleb moving, it is exactly 7:23 p.m. when I start running water down the sink. I quickly find my hidden razor blade and at 7:27 I carefully slice into my right arm. About halfway up this time. It's my second cut today. At this rate, I don't think I'll ever be able to stop.

But the rush of relief is worth it. The disaster that is my family just fades away and I feel that I have control again. And I can breathe again. It's just me and my wound and my blood, alone in the bathroom. Why does this feel so good?

six

CALEB NEVER CAME HOME LAST NIGHT. AND MY DAD ALREADY LEFT, I ASSUME for work, by the time I got up this morning. The house is still and quiet and, I can almost make myself believe, peaceful. But it's a false sort of peace. A temporary illusion.

One benefit of Caleb's absence is that I have the bathroom all to myself this morning. I can shower for as long as I like. I'm careful as I rub soap over my recent cuts. They're still pretty raw and sore. But even though it stings, the cleansing feels good, and I imagine that it will help them heal. I assure myself that I won't cut again today. And maybe not tomorrow either. I remind myself that tonight is the art fair, and this has the potential to be a really good day. I can make it a good day.

Because Caleb isn't around to pester me, I spend as much time as I want in front of the bathroom mirror. I even take the time to blow-dry my hair. And instead of braiding it as usual, I let it hang loose down my back. Abby says I have the best hair. A deep, almost-black shade of brown, it's thick and heavy and straight. I don't usually bother to dry it since it takes forever. But today I think it may be worth it. And, okay, I still remember how Kelsey draped herself over Glen's art project yesterday, her blonde hair falling all over the place. Not that I plan to imitate her, but I don't see how it could hurt anything to wear my hair down for a change.

I take extra time to put on mascara, a little blush, and some lip gloss. It's not much, really, but it does improve things. Then I stare at myself in the mirror with my towel wrapped around me like a sarong. If I stand far enough back and squint just a little, I almost don't notice the dark lines and welts that cover my arms. I can almost imagine they're not there. But then I open my eyes wide and look. They are still there. Red and ugly and telling.

Don't think about it. I go back to my room. *Someday this will all just be a memory.*

According to my radio, today's weather forecast is for "warm and sunny, heading into the low eighties." Even so, I know I'll wear a long-sleeved top. But today I pick one that's lighter weight. It's a white linen shirt with shell buttons up the front and on the cuffs. I got it on sale at Banana Republic last summer. Funny that I knew to buy long sleeves back when I wasn't even cutting yet.

First I put on a pale blue camisole that's got a little lace in front, and then I layer the shirt over that, taking care to button the cuffs. I don't want them slipping up my wrists. There can be no cutting today. One drop of blood on this shirt will shout my issues to the world. And since I plan to remain at school until the art fair begins—I promised Mr. Pollinni that I'd help with setup—there won't be time to come home and change in between. I decide to forgo my usual overalls, opting instead for a short denim skirt that I haven't worn in ages. And I go barelegged. One of the benefits of my Native American heritage is that my legs have enough color to pass for a tan even when they haven't been in the sun for months. I promise myself, not for the first time, I will *never* cut on my legs. I've read on websites that some girls cut all over their bodies. I am determined not to cut anything but my arms. And I plan to stop doing that *immediately*. Today is a brand-new day.

I look at my reflection in the mirror one more time and think I look almost normal. Then I add some beaded earrings and a necklace that I made last winter, back before my mom got sick, when I was still into beading. I used five shades of blue, and the set actually looks pretty good. Abby thinks I have a knack for putting beads together. I gave her a similar set for her birthday, except in shades of pink, and she wears it all the time and even gets compliments on it.

It's still early enough to have some breakfast. I usually skip it, but since I'm trying to do today right, I have a glass of orange juice and a piece of toast. And then I write a very specific note to my parents, reminding them about the art fair tonight, and how I won't be home until late. I even invite them to come, though I don't really expect to see them there. They haven't been out together in a long, long time.

At just a few minutes past eight, I finally see Abby's car pull into the driveway. We have this little unspoken agreement that she's to wait out there for me, without honking, and I will get out of the house as fast as possible without having Daddy Dearest running interference.

Abby is one of the few people outside my immediate family who has actually witnessed my dad losing it. Of course, he made a remarkable recovery when he realized I had a friend in the house. He even joked with her about how cranky parents can get sometimes. I was grateful that she didn't buy it, and that she didn't make a big deal about it either. I haven't told her everything about my family, but she knows enough to be fairly understanding. And, thankfully, she knows enough to keep her mouth shut.

"Whoa, girlfriend," she says when I climb into her Bronco. "You're looking pretty good today."

I kind of smile. "Thanks."

"What's the occasion? Or, let me guess, you finally figured out that Glen really is into you and you've decided to play along? Baiting the hook, are we?"

"No. I just wanted to look nice for the art fair tonight."

"Oh." She's clearly disappointed.

"Okay, and I guess I don't mind if Glen notices."

She laughs. "That's better. I was starting to get worried about you."

I glance at her. She almost sounded serious. "Huh?"

"Well, you know, what with the way you've been dressing lately . . . and how you've been acting . . . I guess I thought you might've been depressed or something."

"Oh."

"But now you're giving me hope, girlfriend."

I smile. "Good. I'm feeling a little hopeful myself."

And, amazingly, that's sort of how my whole day goes. Maybe it's because I look better than usual, or maybe I am actually smiling for a change, but it's like everyone is being a whole lot nicer to me than they normally are. By lunchtime I get to thinking that I've cleared some major kind of obstacle in my life, and I'm thinking this really could be the big day—the day I quit cutting myself for good. I'm more hopeful than ever before.

Even Glen seems more interested in me. We chat like old buddies at lunch then even hang together during art. Nothing anyone would really notice—except for me—but it feels like something's happening. And maybe Kelsey is a little jealous.

"Hey, Ruth," Mr. Pollinni approaches my table just before class ends. "Can I ask a favor of you, for the art fair?"

"Sure," I tell him. "What is it?"

"Well, I had Claire Engstrom down for the pottery demonstration from seven to eight, but she's home with the flu. Do you think you could take her place?

"I guess so. But I might be kind of rusty. I haven't done much pottery this term."

Pollinni laughs. "I doubt it, Ruth. The last time I saw you throw a pot, I don't think you even had your eyes open."

Well, I seriously doubt that. Although pottery is more about feeling than seeing. Even so, I'm feeling a little nervous about agreeing to do this. I might screw up in front of everyone. I feel a familiar tightening in my stomach. The gnawing fear that I might fail, that I'll blow it and end up looking stupid. I hate looking stupid. Why did I agree to do this?

"Something wrong?" Glen asks as we're leaving art.

I shrug.

"Come on. Tell me."

"It's no biggie," I say. "I'm just a little uncomfortable about throwing pots in front of everyone. I mean, what if I mess up?"

He laughs. "Then you mess up—and just start over again."

"Easy for you to say."

"How about this," he says. "What if we split up the shift? You throw for half an hour and I'll do the next one."

"You do pottery?"

He grins and nods.

"A man of many hidden talents . . . "

"You should talk."

So now I'm feeling a little bit better. And it's sweet that Glen wants to help me with this. I think maybe he does like me. And so the day progresses, and I'm really feeling like I've almost got the upper hand on my life now. Like things are finally going forward, and maybe I'm really going to make it.

It's a mad rush to get everything set up after school. But about a dozen of the art students, including Glen and me, are really taking tonight seriously. Mr. Pollinni has it completely worked out—where everything should go, and exactly how it should all look. When we're done, I'm impressed.

The cafeteria looks as if it's been transformed into a real gallery. Even the lighting, brought in by one of Pollinni's talented friends, looks great. All the outside signs are in place and there's a café-like area with desserts and coffee for sale and a section where student art, as well as some that's been donated by local artists, is for sale. He even lined up a small jazz ensemble to play background music.

"Everything looks great!" I tell Mr. Pollinni. "And we have time to spare."

Altogether there are about twenty art students scattered at stations throughout the cafeteria so we can demonstrate our skills. I already set up my easel in a somewhat out-of-the-way corner. I plan to do an acrylic demonstration (that is, if I survive my stint on the potter's wheel). I notice that Glen is setting up his easel right next to mine. He's going to be working on a charcoal drawing tonight.

"You ready to hit the wheel?" he asks as I lay several tubes of paint out in a fan around my palette.

I glance up at the clock to see it's about ten minutes until seven. "Guess I better go for it," I say as I pick up my paint smock, which is actually just an oversized flannel shirt that I scavenged from my dad last year.

"Break a leg." He winks at me.

"Right."

"Just relax, Ruth, you'll be fine."

"Thanks." I'm thinking that if I hurry, I might actually get in a few minutes of warm-up time before anyone gets here. So I wave good-bye and head over to the wheel. It's in a fairly open area right next to the entrance, like it's the main event. Just what I need.

I try not to think about that as I tie back my hair and pull on my smock. I use a wire to cut several blocks of clay and begin slapping the pieces around until they're all bubble-free and lined up and ready to throw. Then I pick up the first slab and slam it into the metal surface of the wheel with an air of confidence that is only skin-deep. But at least I hit dead center. That's always a good start.

So far, so good. I turn on the electric wheel, dip my hands in water, and the next thing you know I'm off to the races. And it's funny; as I sit there really getting into it, my hands working the smooth, wet clay, absorbing its coolness and feeling it take shape beneath my fingers, I hardly notice that people have begun to trickle in. Several grade-schoolers are standing around the fast-moving wheel watching me work.

"Cool," says a blonde girl who looks to be around ten or so. "I wish I could do that."

I look up and smile at her. "You can. Just start taking art in middle school. They do pottery there."

"Really?" Her eyes are wide.

I nod. "That's where I started."

The spectators all *ooh* and *ah* as I make a small indentation on top of the spinning ball, opening it up into what is quickly becoming a pot. Then I pull it up taller, creating a slender cylinder, and this impresses them even more. Really, I suppose it does look like magic to them. To my surprise, it's actually kind of fun. I'm really getting into this!

"Looking good, Ruth," says Glen from behind me. "You sure you want to give this up?"

"Is it time?" I ask.

"You've got about five more minutes." Then he leans down. "Hey, you're getting your sleeves all messy."

I look down and see that the cuffs of my nice white blouse are totally splattered with the reddish-brown clay.

"Here, let me help you."

I take in a quick breath. "It's okay. Just leave it—"

But it's too late, he's already reached down for my right hand, like he's going to push up my sleeve for me. With pounding heart, I jerk my hands off the pot so quickly that I accidentally knock it and it warps—badly. Thrown off balance, it flops over and looks as if it's been murdered. The spectators make disappointed noises.

"Bummer!" says a middle-school boy.

"Sorry," Glen tells me, moving away from me now. "I was just trying to—"

"It's okay," I say quickly, standing and grabbing for a rag to wipe my hands. "You just startled me is all."

"Sorry," he says again, looking uncomfortable.

"It's fine," I say in a stiff voice. "Why don't you go ahead and take over now?"

"Hey, Ruth, I'm really—"

But I'm already walking away. I cannot take this! I head straight for the bathroom, holding back tears of humiliation. I rinse the remaining wet clay from my hands, washing and washing even after they are clean. When I look up into the mirror, I can see that my face is flushed and blotchy. And my shirt sleeves are a total mess. I'm a mess. Why did I think I could do this? I am so stupid! So clueless. Such a total loser. What makes me think I can pull off a normal life? I feel so frustrated now that all I want to do is go get my backpack, find my Altoids box, and escape all this. Escape this pathetic excuse of a life.

seven

NO, RUTH, I TELL MYSELF AS I STARE AT MY REFLECTION IN THE MIRROR. AND then I imagine myself sliced up like I've been through a giant shredder, not just my arms, but my face and the rest of my body too. I imagine myself bleeding all over the place. This has to stop. I can't let a little thing like Glen trying to pull up my sleeve totally undo me like this. I have to just shake this thing off and move on.

So I try to rinse the splattered clay out of my shirt cuffs, but I only make a worse mess. Instead of just being splattered, they're soaking wet and a light shade of orange now. I blot them as dry as I can with paper towels, then force myself to go back out to the art fair. I can't give up.

At least my pottery session is done. And despite the strong urge, I didn't resort to cutting. That's something. So I go back to my easel, congratulating myself for being strong, and start to paint. I've got a postcard of a lighthouse draped in fog taped to the corner of my canvas. It's mostly shades of gray and blue. So the only paint colors I need seem to be black and white and blue. I squirt generous dollops of those onto my palette. And I begin to paint. Something about the sparseness of the colors pulls me in, and it's not long before I start to lose myself as I move the paint across the canvas, blending and shading to get the fog just right.

"Sorry I messed you up," says Glen as he returns to his easel and picks up a piece of charcoal.

"I'm sorry I overreacted," I tell him, paintbrush poised in midair as I study how the trail of light from the lighthouse penetrates the fog.

"I should know better than to sneak up on an artist at work."

I want to say something more, to reassure him that it wasn't his fault, that it was me and my own stupid hang-up. But what can I really say without exposing what a loser I am? "Did T. J. take over the wheel?" I ask absently.

"Yeah. But, between you and me, I think he could use some practice."

I laugh. "Just don't tell him that."

"That's a pretty depressing scene, Ruth."

I glance up, stunned to hear my dad's voice. He's wearing a slight frown as he looks at my canvas.

"You came!" I say when I recover enough to find my voice. And not only did my dad come, but to my totally shocked surprise, my mother is with him. I just stare at her—like I've never seen this woman before in my life. She looks shorter than usual, or maybe I have grown since last winter. And her denim jacket, which I always thought looked so cool on her, seems to swallow her. At least she has combed her hair and pulled it back into a silver barrette. Even so, her eyes have that vacant expression, as if she's not really present. Sometimes, like now, I am certain that she's gone. Maybe for good.

"Mom," I say as I step over and take her hand. "I can't believe that you came. Are you feeling okay?"

A faint smile. Or perhaps a shadow of one from long ago. She nods. "I'm okay." Then she seems to study my painting. "I like it," she finally says.

Glen has come over, and I have no choice but to introduce him to my parents. I also mention the fact that he's the one who gave me a ride home yesterday. To my relief, he shakes both my parents' hands. He is very cordial and polite, and I see no reason that my dad should find any fault with him.

"So you're an artist too," my dad says, using his public voice now. "Let's see what you're working on." He steps over and looks at the charcoal sketch. It's the beginning of an old pickup, and really quite good. "Hey, I used to have a truck almost like that," my dad tells him. "Fifty-four Ford?"

"Yep."

Dad nods and rubs his chin, smiling just like he's a normal guy, a good ol' boy that you can count on when times are tough. Yeah, sure. "Mine was red. Bright candy-apple red. Painted it myself. And rebuilt the engine too. Wish I still had that old truck. She was a honey."

Glen is smiling and I think I can see the wheels in his brain turning. I'm sure he's thinking that my dad's just fine, perfectly normal, and my mom is the real problem. She certainly looks like a problem as she hovers near me, glancing nervously around the crowded, noisy room as if someone in here might be armed and dangerous, out to get her.

I'm so relieved when my parents finally leave. I try to get back into my painting, but it's like something in me just broke. Like I don't even know how to paint anymore. So I just stand there, holding my paintbrush close to the canvas and pretend to be working. I'm actually just spacing and wishing I could get out of here. Wishing I could just disappear. Wishing I were alone with a razor blade. *I am so pathetic.*

Finally it's over. Glen is driving me home. But I feel numb and tired and my stomach is tied in a square knot.

"You're awfully quiet, Ruth."

He's sitting behind the wheel, waiting for the light to turn green. I take a deep breath, force a smile for him. "Sorry."

"Everything okay?"

I shrug. "I guess I'm just worn out from the art fair and everything. It's been a long day."

"Yeah. But I think it went really well tonight. Pollinni was sure happy with how many people showed up."

"Yeah, he said we made some pretty good money, too."

"And you can't be too disappointed about the awards, Ruth. You got more than anyone else."

"You didn't do too badly yourself," I say, trying to sound like a normal girl.

"Well, for the new kid anyway."

"And it was cool meeting your mom," I tell him. "She seems really nice." His mom had shown up during the last half hour with sparkling blue eyes and a great smile.

"Yeah, she's okay."

But I can tell by the way he says "okay" that he really likes her. And I could tell by the way he introduced her tonight that he was proud to call her his mother. I wish I could've felt that way about mine.

"Your parents seemed nice too." But his tone is unconvincing and I can tell he's just being polite.

I sort of laugh. "You really think so?"

"Your dad was pretty friendly."

"Yeah, well, he had on his party face. Trust me, he's not always like that."

"Your mom was pretty quiet."

"She's had a hard year."

"Oh."

"But it's probably a good sign that she came. She hardly ever leaves the house." I sigh. "She wasn't always like that, Glen."

"You mentioned how your dad kind of got to her last year, and that she kind of fell apart. But what happened exactly?"

I really do want to tell him the details, and I wish I could just pour it all out. But where do I begin? I'm not even sure I know exactly what happened myself. "It's a long story," I finally say. "The short version is she's not herself anymore."

"Is that going to change?"

I shrug. "I don't know."

"Is she getting help?"

"You mean, like a shrink?"

"Yeah, or counseling . . . you know."

"She did at first. But then our insurance quit covering it and my dad thought it was just a waste of time and money."

"Oh."

And here's what's weird. I don't tell Glen this, but I kind of sided with my dad on that one at the time. I thought, *Why can't Mom just pull herself back together*? Like, how hard can it be to get out of bed, do a little housecleaning, get some groceries, do some laundry? And while she does some of these things some of the time, Caleb and I do most of it.

"Did I tell you my brother ran away last night?" I'm not sure if I'm trying to change the subject or just suddenly worried about Caleb.

"Seriously?"

"Yeah. He and my dad got into it pretty good. And then Caleb just walked out."

"Do you know where he went?"

"Probably a friend's house."

"Is he going to be in trouble?"

I slowly exhale as I consider this. "Yeah, you could say that."

Glen pulls into my driveway now. "Well, hang in there, Ruth."

"Thanks," I tell him. "And thanks for the ride."

"No problem." He smiles. "Any time."

"See ya." I hop out and head toward my house. I have no idea what will happen once I open the door, but I suspect it won't be good. I can hear yelling inside. I pause, trying to appear as if I have a key that I'm using to unlock it, but I'm really just giving Glen time to drive away. When he's gone, I slowly open the door.

"What do you mean you're not coming home?" my dad is screaming into the phone. "You're fourteen, Caleb. This isn't your decision. You want me to call the police?" He pauses and I attempt to tiptoe past him. "You keep this up, Caleb, and you're going to end up in juvi court—and worse!" He slams the phone down and turns to me.

"What're you sneaking around for?"

I stop just a few feet from my bedroom door. "I didn't want to disturb—"

"What is with you kids?" Dad yells at me. "Sneaking around, running away from home, acting disrespectful. What is wrong with kids these days?" And then he lets loose with word after word, sentence after sentence of ranting and raging. I don't even know how he can go on for so long. How is he able to come up with all this stuff? Most of his words go right over me. But some of them hit their target. Words like "stupid" and "loser" and "useless" seem to stick. Those are the kinds of words that come back and taunt me later.

"You're just like your mother!" he finally screams. As if that should explain everything. "A useless squaw who's as cold as a fish.

Get out of here, Ruth! I can't stand to look at you."

And so I slink into my bedroom, silently close the door, and wait. It's not long before his pickup roars to life and then tears off down the street.

This day started out so good. Everything was going so well. I really believed that I could get through it without cutting. Maybe I still can. Maybe if I just breathe deeply and think positively, maybe I can get through this.

But after a few minutes, I know that I can't. It's like I'm going to burst. The pain is all around me — inside and out — and all I want is an escape. Just a little escape.

I move silently to the bathroom and get out my razor blade. *Just one more time.* I lower the blade to an uncut space on my right arm. *Then I'll get better. Just one more cut. I need some relief. I need to be able to breathe again.*

I slice across my arm. Perhaps a little more deeply than necessary, but it's high enough up that I'm sure I didn't cut any main arteries. The blood oozes out quickly and I have to scramble to grab a towel before it drips on the floor. I press the hand towel onto my wound and sink into a crouched position, leaning my back into the cold porcelain of the tub. At least I can breathe now.

Maybe tomorrow. Maybe I can quit this thing tomorrow.

eight

"So what's going on with you and Glen?" Abby asks me on the phone the next morning.

"I don't know." I turn on the dishwasher. It's Saturday and I'm trying to get all the chores done before my dad comes home from work, which is at one on Saturdays.

"Come on," she urges as I wipe the countertops with the dishrag. "Tell me what's going on."

"He's cool," I say as I scrub the stove top, careful to get the deepest grooves clean. My dad will check.

"Yeah, I know he's cool. But is he *into* you?"

"I really don't know. I mean, he's nice to me, and I think we're friends. But that's all I can say right now, Abby."

"Are you into him?"

I consider this as I rinse the dishrag in hot water, balancing the phone between my shoulder and head as I squeeze the excess water out. "I guess so."

"Well, I think he's into you too," says Abby. "I saw him watching you last night. You were painting and he was just staring at you like he couldn't get enough."

"Seriously?" I pause from wiping down the front of the refrigerator. "He was really watching me like *that*?"

"Yeah. I think he really likes you."

I feel a warm rush of excitement. But at the same time I'm almost afraid to get my hopes up. Like, what if Abby's wrong or just trying to be nice? I mean really, why would someone like Glen like someone like me?

"So aren't you happy, Ruth?"

"Yeah, I guess."

"*Yeah, I guess?* Can't you do any better than that?"

"What do you want me to do? Jump up and down and scream?"

"Maybe. I'd like to see you get excited about something for a change."

I don't respond to this. Instead I scrub even harder on the fridge, determined to make it shine.

"Want to go to the mall with me today?"

"Sure, but I can't go until I'm done with chores."

"No problem. I don't plan on getting out of bed for another hour or two. How about I pick you up around one?"

"Can you come a little before that?" I'd rather not be here when my dad gets home. I'm sure he's still really irritated about Caleb's little disappearing act. The truth is, I'm irritated too. It means twice as much work for me.

"Sure. How about a quarter 'til? Does that give you enough time to make a safe getaway?"

I kind of laugh. Abby knows me too well. "Thanks. I'll be ready."

And so I have to kick it into high gear. It's about ten now and I still have to vacuum and dust and sweep and take out the trash and about a dozen other time-consuming things. At times like this, I really wish my mom would get up and help out. I know she does a few things while we're at school or in the middle of the night. But it's like she's afraid to come out if anyone is around. Why can't she get over it?

I'm working so hard and fast that I've actually worked up a sweat by noon. I'm just heading for a quick shower when I hear someone coming into the house. Thinking it's my dad, home early, I feel a chill of disappointment run through me. But when I peek around the corner of the hallway, I see that it's just Caleb.

"What are you doing?" I ask as I pull the belt of my bathrobe more tightly around me.

"Just getting some stuff before Dad gets home."

"Where are you staying?"

Caleb scowls. "I can't tell you."

"Why not?" I demand. "What if something happens? What if I needed to get ahold of you? Like what if Mom did something or—"

"Do you swear not to tell Dad?"

I consider this. Caleb and I always take our promises to each other seriously. Even more so during the past six months. "I swear," I finally say.

He studies me as if he's weighing my integrity.

"Caleb," I say with impatience. "If you can't trust me, who—"

"Yeah, yeah. Well, I'm staying with Grandma."

"Grandma Wallace? I'd think she would've called Dad a long time ago."

"Not Grandma Wallace. *Grandma Donna.*"

"Wow." I slowly nod. Grandma Donna is Mom's mom, and not always the most reliable sort of grandma. Although she's pretty interesting. "I thought she moved to Oklahoma with her last husband."

"Well, she's back. And he's not."

"How'd you find her anyway?"

"I called Uncle Rod. He told me where she was staying."

"Where's that?"

"Out on Ferris Road. She's got a trailer out there that her brother is letting her use. She doesn't have a phone, but if you really needed to reach me, I mean like a real emergency, you could call Uncle Rod."

"You live in a trailer? Like the kind people go camping in?"

"No, it's bigger than that. I guess you call it a mobile home."

"What about school?" I don't remind him that his grades are low enough that he could be stuck in junior high for another year if he doesn't straighten up.

"Grandma Donna's neighbor gives me a ride on his way to work."

"How long do you plan to stay there?"

Caleb frowns. "I don't know. All I know is I can't stand it here anymore. I'm afraid I'm going to kill Dad someday."

"*You're* going to kill Dad?" I look at his slender frame. He's barely as tall as I am. And Dad probably makes up about two of him. Murder doesn't seem likely.

"I imagine doing things," he says, "like maybe putting rat poison in his coffee or messing with the brakes on his truck or maybe throwing an electrical appliance into the shower while he's in there."

"Oh." I feel my eyes widen.

"For now I'm staying with Grandma Donna. Until I can figure things out."

"Did you tell her about anything?"

"A little. She doesn't ask too many questions."

"I'll bet."

"Well, I better hurry and get my stuff. My ride's waiting."

I put my hand on his shoulder now. "I miss you, Caleb."

"Yeah." He almost looks like he has tears in his eyes. "I'm sorry to leave you like this, I mean with Dad . . . and everything. But I didn't know what else—"

Then I uncharacteristically hug him. To my surprise, he doesn't resist, although I can tell we both feel uncomfortable when we step apart.

"What is *that*?" he asks suddenly, pointing down at my arm where my bathrobe sleeve has come up to my elbow.

I quickly push down the sleeve without answering him.

But he reaches over and pushes it back up, exposing at least six scars of varying ages. *"Ruth?"* His eyes narrow. *"What's going on?"*

I push it back down and look away. "Nothing."

Then he cusses.

"It's no big deal, Caleb—"

"It figures," he says with real disgust. "This whole family is so messed up—I don't know why I'd think that you should be any different." Then he turns and walks toward his room.

"Caleb," I begin, but I have no idea what I can say to him. I mean, what can I possibly say that will change what he thinks of me now?

"I gotta hurry," he calls back in a husky voice. "I don't wanna be here when Dad gets home." He closes his door behind him.

"You and me both," I mutter as I head for the bathroom.

I pause by the drawer where my razor is hidden. Everything in me wants to go for it now—like a magnet I am drawn to its metallic pull. And why not? It'll only take a few minutes and then I'll feel better.

But somehow I manage to just shake my head and go directly to the shower. *I am not going to cut today. I am not going to cut.* I say this over and over as I take a shower. My cut from last night is still throbbing and it burns when the water hits. It's starting to bleed again, so I have to put a fresh bandage on it when I get out. I have to stop doing this. It's not only hurting me but it's hurting Caleb now too.

Caleb is gone by the time I am dressed. I peek into his room to see that it looks pretty much the same. Neatly made bed. Everything perfectly in its place, the way we've been trained. I check out his closet and a couple drawers. He's taken quite a lot of clothes. As if he plans to be gone awhile. And while I know it's not really my fault, I can't help but feel as if I am partially to blame for this. If only I were stronger, more together.

Don't think about it. There's nothing you can do anyway. I decide to focus on my own life—maybe I can salvage something here and help Caleb later. And for some unexplainable reason, the possibility that Glen might actually like me gives me strength. And I think maybe, just maybe, if something can come of this relationship . . . well, maybe I would get better, get healthy, move on. But what can I do to help facilitate this thing? How do I compete against all the other girls who might like to get their hooks into Glen?

Finally, I decide it's time to clean up my act—to start acting, looking, and even dressing like a "normal" girl. In other words, it's time to do some shopping. And so I decide to take some extra money with me to the mall today. Okay, I know my dad would be furious if he saw me "robbing" my piggy bank, but it is my own money, after all. Some saved from babysitting and some from the meager allowance I'm given each week. But I should be able to use it how I like. Right? Well, if this were a normal family and if I were a normal kid, it would be right. For now, I just have to cover my tracks and hope my dad won't be checking up on my finances anytime soon.

Now I'm thankful that I took the time to make my dad a nice

big tuna-fish sandwich earlier. I wrapped it in plastic wrap and put it in an obvious place in the fridge. I just wish I'd had time to make chocolate-chip cookies or brownies. That might've helped to appease him even more. Then I leave a note, clearly saying what I'm doing (well, other than the spending money part) and who I'm with and when I'll be back. And, not taking any chances, I also mention the sandwich and make a smiley-face picture next to it. Yeah, I'm pretty desperate.

It's getting close to one now, and I'm suddenly worried that Abby will be late and my dad will get here and figure out that Caleb's been here and, well, you just never know which way it might go from there. But then Abby is here, and I'm flying out the door, jumping into her car. With a heart that's pounding I tell her to hurry up and get out of here.

"Free at last," I say, as she drives away from my house. I lean back into the seat of her Bronco and finally breathe.

"Has Caleb come home yet?" She turns a corner that takes a different route to town, one that does not pass by the tire store. I have to give her this much, the girl is thinking. So I tell her about his little appearance, not mentioning his unfortunate discovery, and I even mention that he's staying with Grandma Donna.

"But you can't tell anyone," I say quickly.

"Like I would do that." Then she laughs. "Grandma Donna. I haven't seen that woman in years. How's she doing anyway?"

"I have no idea. I didn't even know she was living around here."

"Remember that time when we went to visit her?"

I nod. Of course I remember. How could I forget? It was the summer before seventh grade, and we decided to ride our bikes out to her place to pick cherries. Somehow we'd gotten it into our heads that we were going to make a cherry pie.

"She was so cute," says Abby. "Trying to get all glammed up for her big date with—what was his name?"

"Mike," I tell her, although I don't say that we later found out that "Mike" was on the lam—wanted for robbery, I think.

Abby goes on, reminding me of how we helped Grandma Donna with her hair and nails and everything, and how she actually looked pretty good for an old lady. But then this Mike dude shows up and he's young enough to be her son and we both suspect that he's probably just using her. But my grandma doesn't even seem to notice. Abby thinks it's all pretty funny, but I mostly think it's pretty pathetic. Like my whole family. Suddenly I feel angry at Grandma Donna too. I wonder why, since she's moved back to the area, she hasn't come around and helped with my mom during these past six months. I heard she visited Mom once in the hospital. But as far as I know that was it. Of course, my dad probably doesn't make her feel too welcome. Everyone knows he can't stand her, or any of my mom's relatives for that matter. We are such a freaking mess.

"Earth to Ruth," says Abby in that obnoxious way of hers, like she thinks she's being clever.

"That's getting old," I tell her. We're just going inside the mall now, but I have obviously not heard a word she's said since we left the car.

"Well, so is your little space-cadet routine, Ruth. I was trying to ask you a question."

"Sorry," I say. "I guess I kinda was someplace else."

"No kidding. *Anyway*, I was just asking if you were hungry, like, should we get something to eat at the food court, or shop first then eat somewhere else later?"

"Your pick," I tell her, even though I think the selection at the food court pretty much sucks.

"Okay," she says. "I vote for the food court. That way we might see someone."

I hadn't really considered this myself, since there's no one I particularly want to see anyway. Well, other than Glen. But then I sort of doubt that he'd come to the mall. Somehow I just don't think he's the type. He'd probably think this was a dumb waste of time. I usually think this myself, but at least it's something to do, and way better than being at home. Besides, Abby loves to shop, and in order to be her friend, I kind of have to play along. Normally, I don't mind trailing her around, although I plan to do some shopping of my own today.

As we head toward the food court, the mere possibility of running into Glen brightens me up some. I'm glad I took time to put on something besides my overalls. Just in case.

But we don't see anyone we know at the food court. We both get a piece of pepperoni pizza and a soda, and then find a table that's in a good location for people watching. Finally, our food is gone, and we give up on seeing anyone.

"We can always come back later," says Abby. "Get some yogurt or something."

"Sounds good." Then I hold up my purse. "And you may be happy to know that I actually plan to shop today."

Her brows go up. "You mean you brought real money?"

I kind of laugh. "Yeah, I thought my wardrobe could use a little boost."

She grabs me by the arm and I try not to wince, but I'm sure it must show. Fortunately she's not looking. "All right then. Let's get going, girlfriend," she says with great enthusiasm.

I take in a deep breath and wish the throbbing pain in my right arm would go away. By the time we hit the first store, it's lessening some. Once again, I promise myself that I will *not* cut again. It's just not worth it. I've got to stop.

"How about this?" asks Abby as she holds up a pale-blue-and-white striped T-shirt for me. "You'd look great in it, and it would go with your beads."

"I'm not sure—"

"Here," she insists. "Just try it on."

So I add it to the several pairs of shorts and jeans that I've already collected. I am trying to focus my shopping on the lower half of my body. Because I know if I pick up a long-sleeved shirt, Abby will make some predictably lame comment about how I always wear long sleeves and it's summer, for Pete's sake. I just am not up for that.

"And how about this?" She holds up a black cami. "You'd look fantastic in it."

So I take the camisole as well. Just to appease her. Or maybe I might wear it underneath something with sleeves, like my linen shirt, if I can get the clay stains out of the cuffs. We both wait in line and finally get into the dressing rooms. I am so glad this place does not allow customers to share rooms!

At first I plan to try on only the jeans and shorts. But one pair of jeans is perfect. In fact they look so great that I'm curious as to how the T-shirt would look with them. So I carefully remove my long-sleeved shirt and slip into the T-shirt. Abby was right. It *does* look good on me. And it fits perfectly. Even so, I could never wear it. Not with these arms. I do my little squint trick where I try to imagine my scars all healed. But it's tough because of the white gauze bandage on my most recent—

"How are you do—"

Abby is hanging like a monkey as she peers over the wall between her dressing room and mine. I feel like someone just slugged me in the stomach. Her expression changes, and she looks just as horrified as I feel.

"Ruth!" Her eyes go wide. "What happened?"

And within seconds she is off the wall and opening the door to my dressing room and staring at my arms.

I feel sick. Literally sick. Like I could lose my lunch right here and now, like I might just puke all over the bright pink carpeting that I'm staring down at to avoid her eyes. I sink onto the padded bench behind me and I just let my ugly, scarred arms hang limply between my legs. What can I say? What can I do? Have I ever felt more humiliated?

nine

"Ruth," Abby says in a quiet voice. "Did you do this to yourself?"

Without looking up, I just nod. I don't think I can speak even if I wanted to. I wish I could just disappear, vanish, cease to exist. Life hurts too much.

Abby puts a gentle hand on my shoulder now. And this gesture alone makes me want to break down and sob. But I won't cry. It's bad enough that she's seen my scars. I can't bear to show her any more of my weaknesses.

"Get dressed," Abby tells me as she picks up my long-sleeved shirt from the floor and hands it to me. "We need to talk."

Then she leaves and I take off the pretty blue T-shirt, hang it back up and, careful of my sore arms, I slip back into the long-sleeved shirt. I take my time putting my khaki pants back on. I hang up the jeans and the shorts and try to think of any other reason to delay what I know is inevitable.

"Are you coming?" Abby calls out.

I emerge with the hangers of clothing. But I'm careful to avoid making eye contact with my best friend. I just want out of here. The sooner the better.

We give the attendant our numbers, put our hangers on the rack by the door, and then walk out, through the store and back into the mall. I consider telling Abby that I have to go now, that I'll catch a bus and see her later—like maybe next year or at our ten-year high-school reunion. But I have a feeling she won't buy that. And so we just walk together in silence.

"Let's get something to drink," she says as we get closer to the food court.

Feeling like a robot or a zombie, I follow her, mimic her order, pay for my drink, then pick it up and follow her to a table in a semi-quiet corner. Then I sit and just stupidly stare at my soda cup. I wish I could think of something witty to say, something that would make this whole thing just blow over and go away. But nothing comes to mind except that I am so stupid. Stupid, stupid, stupid! Just like my dad's always telling me.

"I've read about cutting," she finally begins, speaking slowly, as if she's trying to come up with the right words to lay this ugly thing on the table. "But I never really got it, Ruth. I mean, why would anyone want to intentionally hurt herself?"

I say nothing.

"Like, okay, I've accidentally cut myself when I'm shaving my legs, and, man, it hurts so bad. And that's just a little nick. Why would you want to have that kind of pain on purpose, Ruth? I just don't get it."

I look up at her now. And she does look confused. She also looks perplexed and frustrated and uncomfortable, and something else—maybe angry. Like, not only does she not get me but maybe she'd like to knock some sense into me too.

"It's hard to explain," I finally say, like that should solve everything.

"Well, try." I can tell by her face that she's not about to let this thing go.

So I take a deep breath, hold it for a few seconds, then slowly exhale. "Okay. It's kind of like you're *already* hurting, you know?" I look up at her to see if she's following this and she nods like she does know. "Like you're hurting so much on the inside . . . but it just won't go away . . . and you don't know what to do with it . . . you know?"

She nods again. "Yeah, I've felt like that sometimes. Like last winter when Derrick broke up with me and I thought I was going to die from the pain."

"Yeah, kinda like that."

"But I don't see how cutting myself would've helped anything."

I nod. "I know. I guess it doesn't really make sense, does it?"

"No. It doesn't. And you have to stop doing it, Ruth. You have to stop doing it *right now.*"

I wish it were that simple. Like I can stop just like that. "I know," I say to pacify her. More than anything else right now, I don't want her to be mad at me.

"So you will?" She looks slightly hopeful now.

"I *want* to stop doing it," I confess. "I really do."

She seems to relax a little. "Good. So, you will stop it then?"

I touch my right arm, going to my most recent cut. My fingers trace the shape of the bandage through the fabric of my shirt, and as usual this brings the confusing sensation of comfort and guilt with it. "Yeah," I tell her. "I'll stop doing it."

"Because it's really freaky, Ruth. It scares me."

"Yeah, I know."

"I mean, I couldn't believe it when I saw your arms. I couldn't believe that anyone could actually do that to themselves. I actually thought at first that maybe your dad did it to you. Like maybe you were a victim of some weird kind of abuse or something."

I don't know what to say now. I'm still embarrassed and uneasy, and Abby continues to talk about cutting. Like it's some kind of therapy for her to go on and on about it, like she needs to get what she saw in the dressing room out of her system. Like someone who's just witnessed a train wreck and can't stop talking about it, like, "Did you see all the blood? Did you hear the screams of the injured people?"

So I just sit there and take it. I nod and I say "I know, I know" about a hundred times. And finally I can't stand it anymore.

"Can we talk about something else now?" I ask. I want to say, "Don't you think that I've been punished enough for this?" But I don't. I know this is all my fault.

She looks a little surprised. "Well, yeah. Sure. Fine."

Then there's this long uncomfortable silence and I know we're not through with this yet. "This isn't easy for me," I finally say. "And it's not like I wanted you or anyone else to know. I mean it's pretty humiliating."

Her expression softens a little. "Yeah, I can imagine."

"And I don't want you to tell anyone, Abby. You won't, will you? I mean not even your mom, okay?" I know how close Abby is to her mom. She tells her almost everything. Well, at least everything about her friends. I doubt she tells her everything about herself.

She seems to consider this.

"Abby? You cannot tell anyone. I mean it. You're my best friend and I have to be able to trust you with this. Okay?"

"Well," she begins slowly. "How about if I make a deal with you? If you really quit doing it, I promise I won't tell anyone. Okay?"

My first response is to get mad. What right does she have to put this kind of pressure on me? This is my problem, not hers. But then I think maybe this is just what I need. Maybe Abby's pressure will help me to actually quit. "Okay," I finally tell her. "I really do want to stop doing this. And if you promise not to tell, I promise not to cut again. Deal?"

"Deal." Now she looks seriously relieved. "That's all I want you to do, Ruth. I mean, you're my best friend and I really do care about you. But I can't handle this cutting business. I mean, really, it totally freaks me out. To imagine you doing that—that—" she kind of gasps. "I mean, it's so horrible. Please, don't ever do it again. I can't take it. Okay?"

"Okay," I say. "And I know it's horrible. Now can we *please* talk about something else?"

"Yeah. Sure."

"Better yet," I say. "Why don't we go back to the Gap so I can get those jeans and those shorts if they're still there? I really liked them."

"Okay. And how about that T-shirt, Ruth?" She looks really hopeful now. "I mean I know it looked pretty bad today, but it could be something you'd wear later on, like this summer, after your cuts heal up and everything. They will heal up, won't they?"

"Sure," I tell her as if I know all about it. "And if I get a tan on my arms, you might not even notice them at all." Of course, I have no idea whether this is true. Some of my scars are six months old and I can still see them. But right now I'll say anything to get Abby to move off this subject. I'm even willing to buy that blue T-shirt if it will only shut her up.

I guess shopping really is good therapy, because by the time we finish, Abby is acting like her old self again. And she's so excited about some of her purchases that she seems to have almost forgotten about my "little problem."

Just as we're leaving the mall, her cell phone rings and she answers it. "Glen?" she says with a surprised expression. I feel a sudden jab of jealousy. Like why is Glen calling Abby?

"No, that's okay," she tells him in a very sweet voice. "As a matter of fact, Ruth just happens to be with me right now. Do you want to talk to her?" Then she hands the phone over to me.

"Hello?" I'm confused.

"Hey, Ruth. Sorry to call you like this, I mean, on Abby's phone. But I tried your house and no one answered. And Finney gave me Abby's number and—"

"That's okay. What's up?"

"I, uh, I wanted to know if you were busy tonight."

"Tonight?" I echo.

"Yeah. I wondered if you'd like to go to a movie or something."

"A movie?" Okay, I realize I sound pretty much like an idiot now, repeating everything he says. But the truth is, I am caught so off guard. I mean, as embarrassing as it sounds, I haven't really dated. And I know my dad isn't too crazy about the idea of my going out with boys. So it's not like I've pushed it or anything.

But Abby is nodding and smiling at me, wildly mouthing the word *yes, yes*, over and over.

So I finally say, "Sure, Glen, that sounds cool. What time?"

He tells me he'll pick me up around seven, and I hang up and hand the phone back to Abby. I'm kind of dazed.

"Why were you stringing him along like that, Ruth?" She shoves the phone back into her bag. "I mean, why didn't you just say yes when he asked?"

"I don't know . . ."

Then she smiles in that coy way of hers. "Oh, I get it now. Playing hard to get, huh?"

I shrug. "Actually, I'm not sure what my dad will say about it."

"Oh."

"I mean, it's not like it's really come up before, you know."

"But you're sixteen, Ruth. You're old enough to go out."

"Maybe according to you."

"You really think your dad will say no?"

I sigh. "I'm not sure what he'll do. But he's not exactly in a wonderful mood since Caleb left home. The timing's not the greatest, you know?"

She seems to ponder this as she digs in her bag for her car keys. "Hey, maybe it would help if I came in with you. Kind of soften him up, you know? You could bring it up while I'm there. He's usually pretty nice to me."

I actually consider this idea. And, while she's partially right—I mean, my dad might act nice when she's around—I can imagine him going totally nuts after she leaves. He'd accuse me of using her to get to him, and it would just get uglier and uglier.

"That's okay," I tell her as we get in her car. "I better do this on my own."

If shopping didn't do it, this new topic of me going out with Glen has really distracted her from the cutting. And to my relief, she doesn't bring it up again. In fact, I have a feeling that she'd just as soon forget about it. I know I would. So we discuss what I'll wear, how I'll do my hair, and important stuff like that.

But the whole time I'm wondering if my dad will throw a fit and put his foot down. And if he does, what will I tell Glen?

"I don't even have his phone number," I say suddenly.

"Whose?"

"Glen's. What if my dad says no? I'll have to call Glen and cancel."

"It'll be on my caller ID. Get my phone out and write it down."

And so I mess around with her phone until I finally figure out how to get the number, then I write it down on my palm. I hope I won't need it. But it does feel good to see those seven digits clearly printed on my hand. Glen's phone number.

My dad's truck isn't in the driveway when Abby pulls in. It's always a relief to get into the house before he does. Especially today, when I've got this bag from the Gap that I seriously don't want him to see. I have no doubt he would insist on plowing through it if he were home. I already hid the receipt in the bottom of my purse so he won't know how much I spent. But it wouldn't surprise me if he removed each item, one at a time, examining the price tags and doing his own mental math. Then I'd not only get a serious lecture on wasting money, but he'd probably drive me back to the mall and force me to return everything. How humiliating would that be?

I thank Abby for the ride and promise to e-mail her after I get home from my date with Glen, that is, assuming I get to go. "Either way, I'll let you know," I say.

"Good luck!"

I hurry into the house, taking my bag straight to my bedroom. I quickly remove the tags, put away the clothes, then stash the bag way back in my closet to deal with later. It's almost five and I figure I might have time to do a few things to help butter up my dad. I start by making chocolate-chip cookies, his favorite, even chopping and adding walnuts just the way he likes them. I check to see if he ate his tuna sandwich. It's gone. A good sign.

Then I go around and straighten up our already spotless house. Everything looks pretty good. I don't see anything that should set him off. As bad as I feel about having Caleb gone, at least I don't need to worry that he's left his muddy soccer shoes by the back door or something. Even so, I check, just to be sure. Then I go outside and actually sweep off the walk and pull a couple of stray weeds from the bare flower bed. I absently wonder who will plant flowers this year. Mom always did that in the past, and I sure can't imagine her doing it now. Maybe we'll just go without flowers this year. It seems fitting.

I go back inside and start getting ready for my date. The house smells good from the plate of still-warm cookies that I've placed very visibly in the center of the kitchen counter. But now I'm starting to worry. What if Dad doesn't come home in time for me to get permission to go out tonight? What do I do then?

I slip on the new jeans and stand before the full-length mirror to admire how perfectly they fit from all sides. I'm tempted to wear the new blue T-shirt too, with a jacket over it, of course. But what if I get too hot? I'll be stuck wearing a jacket all night long. Besides that, I think this blue T-shirt should be incentive to reach my no-more-cutting goal. I will wear it when my scars have faded and after I've managed to get tan enough to cover them up. Maybe I'll even try some self-tanning cream, if I can keep it from looking streaky and fake.

Finally I decide on a long-sleeved black T-shirt that looks pretty good with my new jeans. I put on silver hoop earrings and minimal makeup, since I don't think I look good with too much anyway. Also, it really bugs my dad. And I don't need him calling me any bad names or sending me off to wash my face—tonight of all nights.

I look outside. Still no sign of Dad. I realize that I haven't heard a peep from my mom, not that it's so unusual for her. But what if something is wrong? What if she did it again, tried to kill herself, I mean? Or what if something happened to Caleb? Feeling seriously freaked, I hurry to Mom's room, knock on the door, and then go in. But there she is, just sitting in her glider rocker, the homely old afghan around her shoulders, and a blank stare on her face. The blank expression is quickly replaced with one of surprise.

"Sorry to burst in on you like this," I say, "but I wondered where Dad is."

"He went out."

"Did he say where?"

She seems to think about this, almost as if she's not sure or can't remember. "He's looking for Caleb," she finally says. But she shows no emotion. Shouldn't she be concerned that her fourteen-year-old son is missing? And does she have any idea that he's with her own mother? Her mother, who she hasn't seen in months? Apparently not. I'm not about to tell her either. After all, I promised Caleb I wouldn't tell Dad. And there's no telling whether our mother could keep that a secret. She's not exactly reliable these days.

"Well, I was going to go out . . . " I begin, wondering why I'm even bothering.

"Just leave a note."

"Okay." I slowly nod. "That's what I'll do." And so I go out and write a note to Dad. I tell him that I already talked to Mom and she said to leave him a note — like that will get me off the hook. Then I tell him that I'm going to a movie with Glen (it's no use to lie; he'll just find out and then be really angry), and I tell him when I'll be back and that I hope he likes his cookies.

I even sign it "love Ruth" and draw another stupid happy face. Man, I am so pathetic. But, hey, whatever it takes, right?

ten

IT'S A GOOD THING I PUT ON PLENTY OF DEODORANT EARLIER, BECAUSE I AM seriously beginning to sweat. I feel like I'm about to pull off some big heist or something. Really, should life be this difficult? This complicated? I'm sure most girls don't have to jump through this many hoops just to go see a movie with a guy. I mean, it's not like we're even serious or anything.

I hear a car pull up. I can tell it's not Dad's pickup because it's not that noisy. To my relief, it's Glen. And instead of letting him get all the way up the walk and into the house, I dash out and meet him midway.

"No one's home," I announce, as if that explains everything.

"You ready to go then?"

I smile at him, hoping to appear casual and relaxed. "Yeah. Sure."

I start to breathe more easily after we're a few blocks away from my house. And that's when I realize I AM ON A REAL DATE. Suddenly I'm a whole new kind of nervous. But at least it's kind of a happy nervous. Not an I'm-about-to-be-yelled-at nervous. Even so, I really don't want to blow things with Glen.

So now I'm wondering—what do you say on a date? Like is there some special way I should talk? And how should I act? I mean, do I wait for him to open doors the way my mom used to do for my dad? He did open the door to his car for me at my house. But what about when we get to the theater? And just because he asked me out, does it mean that he pays for everything tonight? Or do we go dutch? Why did I ever agree to go out in the first place? It's making me into a freaking basket case.

Then I look over at him. He is so cute. And we really do have a lot in common. Then I realize that he actually seems a little nervous too. Could it be?

"I have to admit that I haven't really dated much," I tell him, deciding that honesty might be the best policy for me tonight. Who knows, maybe it will help me to not look so stupid if I'm just upfront about things.

"Don't feel bad. I haven't really dated much either. In fact, I've never even had a real girlfriend. And I'm seventeen. Is that pathetic or what?"

I laugh. "No, I think it's kind of nice. The truth is, I haven't had a real boyfriend either."

"Is it because of stuff with your family?"

"Yeah, pretty much. I mean, my life's complicated already. Why add to it, you know?" Of course, as soon as I say this, I realize it could sound like I'm not interested in him or that I think he's a complication. Not exactly the message I wanted to send.

"I know what you mean."

"Not that I want my life to continue like this," I say quickly. "I'm ready for some changes, even if I have to bring them on myself." I don't tell him that my dad could be going totally ballistic by the time I get home tonight. I'm glad I didn't mention in my note exactly which theater or movie we were going to, since it wouldn't surprise me if Dad showed up and told me to come home. Okay, maybe that's too extreme. He wouldn't want to make a scene like that in public.

Even so, who knows what I'll face when I get home?

"Change is good," he says as he pulls into the newest theater complex. This is the biggest complex in town, and it would be difficult to find anyone in here.

I'm not sure whether I should wait for him to open my door or not, but something in me says to just get out. I mean, how embarrassing would it be if I just sat there and he never came around to open it?

We make small talk as we walk toward the theater. Mostly about last night's art fair and how well it went. I try not to think about how I flipped out when Glen tried to push my sleeve up. Hopefully, he has forgotten all about that. I'm sure he must think I'm fairly neurotic anyway.

He gets in line and I stand next to him, but when we get to the ticket booth, he steps in front of me and purchases two tickets. So, at least I know that's how it goes. One less thing to worry about. Then he asks what I want from the concessions, and I boldly tell him that the popcorn smells pretty good.

"And to drink?" he asks.

"Sierra Mist?" This is weird and foreign to me. And I know how expensive theater food is. Maybe I shouldn't ask for anything. But the truth is, I haven't eaten anything but a couple of chocolate-chip cookies and milk since lunchtime, and I'm kind of hungry. I go and save us a place in the movie line, and before long, Glen is coming my way, carrying one huge bucket of popcorn and two big drinks.

"Thanks," I tell him. As I take my drink, the line starts to move, and before long we're seated in the semidark theater. And as we watch the ads and previews, sharing from the same bucket of popcorn, I actually start to relax.

The movie turns out to be so-so, but we go out for coffee afterward and enjoy totally tearing it apart. It seems we both have strong ideas on what makes a good film. But then I notice the time, remembering that I promised to be home by eleven.

"I kind of have a curfew," I tell Glen. "We should probably go."

"No problem." He smiles at me. "This has been really fun tonight, Ruth."

And so we're driving to my house, and I'm thinking *this really has been fun, but now I might have to pay the price for all this fun.* Or is it possible that this is really my lucky night and my dad has gone out for the evening, either to Jimmy's or The Dark Horse Tavern?

But there his truck is, sitting like a giant red watchdog in our driveway. "You don't need to walk me to the door," I say, glancing at the darkened house to make sure my dad's not lurking somewhere, watching us from between the slits in the blinds.

"Your dad?" he asks.

I nod and reach for the door handle. "Yeah, this is where the whole dating thing gets a little complicated." Then I force a smile. "But I had a really great time tonight, Glen. Thanks so much!"

He looks a little worried, like he's concerned for my welfare or something. "You'll be okay, won't you?"

"Sure. My dad's bark is way worse than his bite." I keep the smile in place. "And, who knows, he might not even bark tonight. I mean, he's met you and he actually seemed to like you." But even as I say this, I know how my dad can put on an act.

Glen seems encouraged by this. "Yeah, your dad seemed cool with everything last night."

"See ya," I say lightly as I get out of the car. "And thanks again. I had fun."

Okay, I wish things were different. I wish he could walk me to the door. Maybe linger a bit, and maybe even kiss me good-night. But while these things may be possible—even for a girl like me—it will probably take time. I need to break my dad into this dating thing slowly, carefully.

I wave to Glen from the front step as he backs out of the driveway, then I quietly open the door and go inside. The lights are off and I think this is kind of odd. But then maybe he's gone to bed. It's possible.

"Where have you been?" His voice booms from the direction of the couch that's in front of the window. I was right. He's been sitting there watching the driveway all the while, just waiting for me to come home so he could lay into me.

I consider turning on a light, then decide that darkness might be better. "I left you a note," I tell him in what I hope is a calm-sounding voice—no traces of guilt to give him something to latch on to.

"A *note*? You think you can just leave me a note then take off, doing who knows what with who knows who, and everything will be okay?"

"Mom suggested—"

"Your mom's out of her head, Ruth! You do not go to your mom for permission to do things you know good and well I will not allow you to do."

"But you weren't here—"

"That's no excuse!" I hear him standing now. "You know that you went behind my back, Ruth. You and your stupid brother—you're both no good. You're both just a couple of good-for-nothing half-breeds who would stab your own father in the back if you got the chance."

His words continue to pummel me, like dull but painful bullets that can't break the skin, but they cut through the heart. It's *half-breed* that I'm stuck on. As best I can remember, he's never used that one before. And the way he said it, spitting it out like it tasted nasty in his mouth, I am sure he meant it. That he believes it. And suddenly I can't take anymore. But instead of saying anything, instead of defending myself, I turn and walk away.

"You do *not* walk away when I'm talking to you, young lady!" He's in a real rage now. His footsteps are coming up behind me, but I run faster, down the hallway and straight to my room. I close the door and then lean against it breathlessly. My heart pounds with as much force as my father pounds against my door as he commands me to come out.

Oh, I know he has the power to break the door down. And maybe that's what I want him to do. Maybe I want him to force his way in here, to raise his fist and to beat me. Just beat me and beat me and beat me. And then, maybe, I would finally have permission, like Caleb, to just leave.

But he just yells and pounds and finally he goes away. And it's not long before I hear the loud roar of his engine and he is gone. How I wish it were for good. How I wish that his pickup would slam into a power pole or drive off a cliff or be run down by a huge semi, and that he would die. I know it's horrible, but it's true. I wish my father were dead. And if I knew how to pray, or if I thought God cared, I would pray for my dad to die tonight.

Instead, I go into the bathroom and break my promise to Abby. I cut myself. Not once. Not twice. But three times. And as I cut myself, I imagine that my sacrifice, my pain, my spilling of blood, might do the trick. Maybe it will get God's attention. Maybe he will kill my dad without me even asking.

eleven

We used to go to church on Sundays. Back when Caleb and I were little and my mom still had some say, we'd all four pile into the family car and go to church together. But then my dad started saying how he needed to sleep in on Sundays—that it was his only day to catch up on his rest. And so my mom would just take Caleb and me. But after a while, Caleb and I followed our dad's example. We wanted to sleep in too. My mom went to church by herself for a while, but finally she just gave up. We haven't been to church for about four years now.

I don't know why I'm thinking about this as I lay in bed this Sunday morning. It's not like I have any intention of going to church today.

My left arm is throbbing from last night's cuts. And I feel ashamed. Like I'm just this hopeless failure. Why should I even bother to try? I am so pathetic.

And at the same time, I'm thinking about what a good time I had with Glen and how much I like him and how I wish he really were my boyfriend. And then I'm thinking about how my best friend, Abby, really cares about me and how much she wants me to quit cutting. And I'm wondering—why isn't that enough? Why can't I keep my promise to Abby? Why can't I care enough about Glen that

I would stop cutting myself? Surely Glen wouldn't want to hook up with a girl who does something like this. If I can't stop this for myself, why can't I stop it for them?

But the truth is, I'm afraid I can't. It's like I don't have any real control. And at the same time, it's like it's my only source of control. And then there's the pain. The never-ending pain that seems only to be diminished by pain. Pain erasing pain. And yet it never really goes away.

Sometimes the only answer seems to be to cut deeper. Cut deep enough to finally end it, to let all the blood drain away so I can rest. And then maybe the pain will finally leave me in peace. Like a long, endless sleep.

I wish I could sleep all day today. But I know that if I'm not out of here, bed made and chores done, I will be hearing about it by the time my dad gets up. And I know that he's home now. I heard his pickup come in around two in the morning. As I expected, God did not strike him dead after all.

So I get up and go through the paces. But even as I do these things, I am asking myself why. Why do I even bother? Why not just stop playing this loser's game? Why not let my dad flip out and beat the heck out of me? Why not just get it over with? Let it all hit the fan? Why not?

The pathetic thing is, I don't even know why not. Maybe it's just the way I've been conditioned. Oh, sure, I may be broken, but it's like I can't operate any other way.

I look at the family computer as I straighten up the den, throwing away old newspapers, picking up my dad's smelly socks. I feel guilty for not e-mailing Abby last night. But how could I? How could I e-mail her about how great the date was and how much I like Glen after breaking my promise to her—times three? I mean, I may be pathetic and stupid and hopeless, but I don't have to be a hypocrite too. A girl has to draw the line somewhere.

I see a shadow of green slipping by—my mom, the green phantom, in her shabby bathrobe. She must've gotten up early, thinking she had the house to herself for a while. But I spoiled it for her. Too bad.

I finish my straightening, quickly eat a bowl of cereal, hiding the evidence of bowl and spoon in the dishwasher. Then, without even writing a note, I leave.

I have no idea where I'm going. Or even why. But I can't stand to be in that house for another minute. It's killing me. My dad is killing me. I am killing me. And I can't take it anymore.

I walk and walk, and before I know it, I'm on the block where my dad's parents live. I must've walked about a mile. Now, I like my grandparents just fine. In fact, they're not very much like my dad—which actually confuses me—but his relationship with them has always been so good that I always feel the need to keep up my guard when I'm around them. Like they might tell on me if I revealed anything about my dad that was questionable. It's weird, I know, but just another part of this weird game I've been taught to play.

"Ruth?" calls a female voice. "Is that you?"

I look over toward the side porch to see Grandma Wallace standing there and shaking out a throw rug. I wave and call hello. "Just taking a walk," I say as I casually stroll up to her.

"Well, for goodness' sake," she says. "Come on in. Can I fix you some breakfast?"

"No, thanks anyway, but I already ate." I follow her as she slowly makes her way into her favorite place, the kitchen. Grandma Wallace is nearly as wide as she is tall, and she loves to feed people.

"How about some coffee then? A donut?"

"Okay," I say as I sit at her kitchen table.

"You still take your coffee with cream and sugar?"

"Uh-huh." I fiddle with the plastic placemats that have been on her table for years now. Each one has a different scene from the Grand Canyon. I suspect she got them at some little tourist shop along the side of the road when she and Grandpa took a trip down there back when I was little. I remember how I wished I could go with them at the time.

She sets a colorful coffee cup in the blue sky above a steep canyon wall, and I briefly wonder why it doesn't fall to the ground.

"How's your mother, dear?" She places a plate of glazed donuts in the center of the table then sets her own cup on a rust-colored mountaintop and takes the seat across from me.

"About the same."

She sighs. "That's too bad."

Now I have a decision to make. Do I keep playing the game, or do I ask if she's heard about Caleb? Feeling just a bit reckless, not to mention hopeless, I go ahead and ask.

Her brown eyes get big with alarm. "Caleb is missing?"

"Well, sort of." Now that the cat's out of the bag, I'm not sure how to play this down.

"What happened?"

I consider my response, fully aware that I could be getting myself into an even bigger mess. I decide that I don't freaking care. "Yeah, he and Dad got into it one time too many," I say in a casual voice, like it's no big deal, like this is something that everyone is aware of.

"One time too many?" Her brows come together. "Meaning they get into it a lot?" I nod without speaking.

"Oh, my."

"But Dad doesn't *usually* hit us. He just yells a lot."

"Well, he's been under a lot of stress since your mother, uh, got sick."

"Oh, this has been going on forever," I tell her. "Dad yells at all of us over everything and anything. I think the reason Mom cracked up was because she just couldn't take it anymore. And that's why Caleb left . . . " *And why I'm so screwed up.*

"Really?" She stands and goes to the stove now, as if she has a pot or something to check there, but there is nothing cooking.

"Yeah. I probably shouldn't have said anything, Grandma, but I guess I'm just fed up too." Now I feel myself starting to choke, and I'm afraid I might cry. I reach over to my left arm and touch the area where I cut myself last night. I press it just lightly enough that the pain brings me back to myself, giving me the strength not to cry. "I don't think I can take it much longer either," I admit.

Then she turns and looks at me, really looks at me. I'm not sure if she thinks I'm lying or if she's just shocked.

"I'm sorry," I say, getting to my feet now. "I shouldn't have dumped this on—"

"No." She holds up her hands. "You sit back down, Ruth. Tell me what's going on. Maybe there's something we can do to help."

So I tell her a little more. Not about my cutting, of course. But I give her more details—about Dad's tirades. About his unreasonable demands. For some reason I want her to know how it feels to live in our house. I want her to feel our pain. And maybe to take some responsibility for it. After all, she and Grandpa raised this cruel man. They must know why he's like this.

"And it just doesn't make sense," I finally say. "I mean you guys don't seem like that at all. I've never heard you or Grandpa say a mean word to anyone. But Dad is so—"

"Let me tell you something, Ruthie." She sits back down and

pulls her chair closer to mine. "Something you should've heard long before now, I'm afraid. But better late than never." She closes her eyes, as if she's trying to pick a place to start. "I'm not your dad's real mother. I married Grandpa when your dad was fourteen. Your dad's real mother had some, uh, mental problems." She shakes her head and sighs. "I actually thought it was such a strange coincidence that your father married a woman with, uh, similar problems—"

"She was fine," I say in my mom's defense. "He *made* her that way. His constant yelling and screaming—nothing ever good enough—"

"I know," she tells me in a soothing voice. "I'm starting to get the whole picture now. Anyway, your father's real mother was very hard on the boys. Not just with her words either. She beat on them on a regular basis."

"Grandpa let her do that?"

"He didn't always know." She shakes her head sadly. "Unfortunately she used your father as her worst whipping boy. Garrett was older and managed to escape a bit more. But one day she beat your father so badly that your grandpa had to take him to the hospital. Well, it wasn't long before everyone knew what was going on, and your grandpa told Marie to leave or face criminal charges. She left."

"Wow," I say, letting this all sink in. I can't imagine anyone, let alone a woman, beating on my dad. It just makes no sense. But then why would Grandma lie? "That is so weird."

"Your grandpa eventually divorced Marie, and I came along a few years later. And, well, we just never felt the need to mention any of this to the grandchildren. Until now, that is."

"Do you think that's why Dad is like that?"

"Well, I don't know much about these things, but I do watch that Dr. Phil on TV, and I suspect he'd think that was the problem with your father. Trouble is, I'm not sure what he'd do to fix him."

"You really think he can be fixed?"

"I don't know, honey. But I sure hope so. In most ways, your daddy is a fine man. I had no idea that things were so messy at home."

"He's good at keeping up appearances, Grandma. And so were we. Well, until Mom lost it. And it seems like Caleb and I have been steadily losing it ever since."

Now she stands up and comes over and hugs me. A soft, warm hug that almost breaks loose the tears. But not quite.

"I'm sorry it's been so hard on you, Ruthie. But things are bound to get better now. Don't you think? I'll talk to Grandpa when he gets back from golfing with his buddies. I'm sure he'll know what to do."

"I hope so. Because, seriously, I feel like I can't take it anymore. And I miss Caleb." I don't mention that I miss my mom too. Somehow I don't think her issues are going to be easy to fix. To be honest, I can't imagine how any of this can really be fixed. But I do feel a tiny bit relieved to hear this story about Dad's childhood. Who would've guessed? And I do plan on sharing this news with Caleb. Not that it will change anything for him. But maybe it'll help him to understand. Maybe that's a beginning.

And so, as I slowly walk home, not overly eager to get there, I tell myself that maybe this is going to change things. Maybe Grandpa can talk some sense into my dad. Maybe things will get better. It could happen.

twelve

INSTEAD OF GOING HOME, WHERE I'M SURE TO GET IN TROUBLE FOR LEAVING without telling my dad, I walk to a convenience store, buy a soda, and make a phone call from the pay phone. I call information and ask for the phone number of Rod Udell, my mom's brother, and wait as they put my call through.

"Hello," says a guy's sleepy voice.

"Uncle Rod?"

"Who is this?"

"It's Ruth. You know, Fran's daughter."

"Oh, yeah. What's up, Ruth?"

"I wanted to get in touch with Caleb. He told me I could find him through you."

"He did, did he?"

"Look, Uncle Rod. Things aren't going too well at home right now. I need to talk to Caleb. I need to tell him something important."

"You sure you're not going to tell your daddy where Caleb is staying?"

"I could've already told him that Caleb's at Grandma's out on Ferris Road. But I didn't. I wouldn't do that."

"Where are you now?"

So I tell him where I am and he says to wait there, and that he'll come and get me. "I need to go out that way anyway," he says.

So I sit down on the curb by the convenience store and wait until an old brown pickup pulls up, making a cloud of exhaust, and my uncle waves from behind the steering wheel. He's wearing a beat-up straw cowboy hat and a friendly grin.

I wave back, surprisingly glad to see him. I think it's been several years now. But for some reason I've always liked this guy. Maybe because he's so laid-back, so totally different from my dad. His black hair is long, pulled back in a tail, and tied with a piece of leather. And he has several tattoos on his arms.

"Hey, you're all grown up, Ruth," he says as I climb into the truck. "You're getting to be a real pretty girl too."

"Thanks," I say, feeling self-conscious.

"You know, your mom was a real beauty when she was younger."

"I know . . ."

"So how's she doing anyway?"

"Not so good."

He frowns. "That's pretty much what Caleb said. I don't see why she doesn't just pack it up and leave Stuart for good. Can't she see that he's no good for her? He's no good for any of you."

"I think she's kind of stuck. I think we're all kind of stuck."

"At least Caleb had the sense to get away."

"But for how long?" I ask. "I mean, Dad's going to find him eventually."

"There are people who can help." He turns onto the highway.

"Like social services?" I ask. "I've heard about how *helpful* they can be."

"You never know. I had a girlfriend once who was a social worker for the state. I know she tried to help people. But it wasn't easy."

I want to change the subject. "Are you still doing your art?"

He nods. "Yep. And music too. My band has been getting some pretty good gigs lately."

"I'm into art too."

"Really?" He tosses me a sideways glance. "Cool."

So I tell him a little about the art fair and the kinds of stuff I really like doing. And he tells me about a mural he's working on. And suddenly I'm thinking, *This feels like family. This feels like what I've been missing.* But my dad has made sure that none of my mom's relatives ever feel comfortable at our house. Mom used to take Caleb and me to visit them, without letting my dad know, of course. But we didn't go nearly as much as we got older. And even less when Mom started getting "sick."

Uncle Rod turns onto Ferris Road, goes about a mile or so, then turns onto another road, this one is gravel. I'm actually trying not to pay too much attention, just in case my dad grills me on where Caleb is. I don't really want to know how to find this place.

Finally we pull up in front of an old mobile home. The kind that is long and narrow and pretty cheesy looking. But there's a covered deck attached to the front and lots of good shade trees around, and I see a barn and what looks like a couple of paint horses back to one side of it. In a way, this whole place is kind of sweet looking. Kinda funky, homey. And I remember now that Grandma Donna always liked horses. My first memory of her is of her putting me on a pony and leading me around in a circle. I think the pony's name was Sugar.

"This is it," says Uncle Rod. "Mom's brother, my Uncle Lane, owns this piece of property. But he's letting her use it for as long as she wants. Needs some work, but it's not too bad."

The inside of the mobile home is shabby but cozy. The furniture is draped in several of the same kind of brightly colored afghan throws that my mom uses, giving the house kind of a carnival feel. My grandma loves to crochet, and she loves wild color combinations. She used to ask me what colors I would want in one, but at the time I wasn't too interested. Maybe I am now. Maybe I'll be like Mom and keep one of Grandma's afghans as a security blanket when my life totally falls apart.

No one seems to be around. "Hello?" calls Uncle Rod.

"Coming," calls a woman's voice from one end of the long, shadowy house. "Is that you, Rodney?"

"Yeah, and I've brought a visitor."

Her dark eyes grow large when she steps out into the living room and sees me. "Frances?" Then she stops and sort of laughs when she realizes it's not her daughter. "Well, of course not. Why, this must be Ruth!" She hurries straight toward me and hugs me tightly against her bony self. Then she holds me back by the shoulders and really looks at my face. "You sure threw me for a loop there, girl. I thought you were my Frances. You look a lot like her, you know?"

"That's what I hear." But all I can imagine is how old and tired my mom looks these days, shuffling around in her grungy green bathrobe, stringy gray hair hanging in her face. Not a pretty picture.

"How is she?" asks Grandma Donna. "Is she okay?"

"Yeah. I mean, she's pretty much the same as when Caleb left. Nothing's wrong, if that's what you mean. I mean, nothing new anyway."

She nods knowingly then sighs.

"Where's Caleb?" I ask.

"Out tending the livestock."

"I saw horses. Is there more than that?"

"Two paints, a couple of steers, several sheep, and too many chickens."

"Wow. How much land do you have?"

"Lane said it's about twenty acres. Not much, but more than enough for an old woman like me."

"I'll go out and let Caleb know you're here," says Uncle Rod.

"Has it been nice having Caleb here?" I ask hopefully. "I mean, is he helping you some?"

She smiles, revealing a missing tooth off to one side. "Caleb's a pure delight. And what a worker. I guess he learned that much from your father." But the way she says this doesn't make it sound like a genuine compliment.

"And you have enough room for him here?" I glance around the small living room.

"I've got two bedrooms. One was full of my junk. But Caleb and I got it cleaned out and moved to a shed out back, and he seems just fine."

"Are you worried about what my dad's going to do?"

She frowns now. "Well, I've wondered if we should call someone." Then she shakes her head. "I wanted Caleb to tell his mother where he was, but he refused. He says she'll tell your dad and that he'll be in bad trouble for sure."

I nod. "Yeah, that's probably true." I'm actually wondering if there's enough room for me to hide out here too. But I know there's probably not. Besides, Grandma Wallace knows what's going on now. She might help to get things changed.

When Caleb comes in, we go out onto the front porch, and I tell him about my conversation with our other grandma. I tell him about what she said about Dad.

"So?" he says finally in a blasé tone.

"Well, I thought you might want to know." I feel slightly defensive. "I thought it might give you some hope."

"Hope for what?"

"That maybe things could change. Maybe Dad will listen to Grandpa and Grandma. Maybe he'll start treating us right."

Caleb kind of laughs now. "You really think so, Ruth? You honestly think that Dad can change?"

I shrug. "I don't know. Why not?"

"I think you're as dumb as Dad says you are." He turns away from me and I suspect he's thinking about my dirty little secret now.

"Thanks a lot." I stand up, mad that he'd say something like that. Especially after I came out here to encourage him.

"Don't get mad at me," he says, standing too. "Dad's the one who screwed everything up."

"But maybe things can get better. I mean if Dad changed, maybe Mom would get well. Maybe we could—"

"Be one big happy family?" He rolls his eyes. "Yeah, right. And maybe we'll win the lottery too. And maybe there's a Santa Claus and an Easter bunny. Get real, Ruth. Nothing's gonna change. And if you're smart, you'll figure out how to take care of yourself before you go down with them."

Now I don't know what to say. I wonder why I even bothered to come out here.

"And just for the record, I am *not* going home." He shoves his hands into his jeans pockets. "I'd rather run away for good and live on the streets. Anything would be better than living with Dad."

"Well, maybe you'll get to stay on here," I say, forcing my voice to be light and positive. "Maybe Grandma Donna can help you figure things out so it'll be legal. And since there's only a couple more weeks of school, you'll have all summer to work things out." I want to add, "And aren't you the lucky one?" I want to let him know that he's not making life any easier for me. And that the anger

Dad used to divvy up between the two of us is totally mine now. But what would be the use? Caleb has obviously landed in a good spot. Why try to take that from him? Besides, maybe I'll have Grandma Wallace to back me now. And Grandpa too. Maybe things are about to get better.

We talk a little more, and I can tell that Uncle Rod is antsy to go. So I tell Caleb I love him and that I hope he can stay on here. Then I hug Grandma Donna again, and I tell her that it might help Mom if she would come visit sometime. "I mean, when Dad's at work," I say quickly.

"Yes," she says sadly. "I'm not stupid, Ruth. I wouldn't dream of coming around when Stuart's at home. That wouldn't help anything."

I feel slightly encouraged as Uncle Rod drives us back to town. I ask him to drop me a few blocks from the house and he just laughs. "Don't want your old man to see who's bringing you home, eh?"

"Well, he might suspect that I've been to see Caleb. He might figure out that you're involved somehow." And while that's partly true, I am actually more worried about myself. I am trying to avoid the tongue lashing I will surely get for having gone someplace with someone from my mom's side of the family. Some Native American heritage might rub off on me, for crying out loud.

To my relief, Dad's not even home when I walk into the house. It's nearly three now, and I suspect I should hang around here and lay low until Dad gets back. Maybe I can pretend like I haven't been gone at all.

Dad gets home around five. As it turns out, he's been over at his parents' house. Apparently they called him when Grandpa got home from golfing, and they have spent the entire afternoon talking. Talking and talking and talking.

Now, if my life was bad *before* I told Grandma Wallace about Dad, it's gone totally to hell now. Not only did Grandpa not say anything to straighten Dad out but the tables have turned, and now everyone thinks I went crying to Grandma simply because I'd been "disciplined" for dating a boy without Dad's permission. That's the picture Dad painted when he went to "smooth things over" with them. Apparently they believed him too, because according to my dad they're now convinced that both Caleb and I are real juvenile delinquents.

"I'm sick and tired of the way you kids are behaving!" Dad yells at me as he storms into the kitchen where I've retreated, thinking he was done lecturing me. But it seems he is only getting warmed up. I lean against the kitchen counter and stare blankly at him, bracing myself for the second half.

"Getting your grandma all worked up over nothing! You should be ashamed of yourself, Ruth. That poor woman already has high blood pressure and diabetes, and now she's sick in bed from all your stupidity."

He shakes his finger in my face now, so close that I can smell the nicotine on it—although he pretends that he doesn't smoke. "I'm warning you, Ruth Anne, don't you go shooting your mouth off to them again—not ever again! It's bad enough your brother's gone missing. I don't need you running around town trying to stir things up, making things worse."

I'd like to say that I was trying to make things better. But I know it's useless. I can't actually speak at the moment, and even if I could, he wouldn't listen.

"And, just in case you didn't know it, you're grounded, young lady! I don't want you going anywhere besides school and home until the school year ends. And you'll be riding the bus from now on.

No more running around with your stupid friends!" He swears now. "It's probably those useless peers that are influencing you like this."

So many things I wish I could say to him. How I'd like to straighten him out. I wish I could yell and scream too. I wish I could tell him that he's a big, stupid jerk and that our messed up lives are all his fault. I wish I were brave enough to ask him how he used to feel when his mother treated him like this—and is he proud of himself for being just like her? But, as usual, I keep my mouth shut so tight that my jaw begins to ache. And then, when he is finally done, I turn and walk away.

And I know where I'm going, I know what I'm going to do. And I just don't really care anymore. Why fight it?

thirteen

IT'S NOT EASY TELLING MY FRIENDS THAT I'M GROUNDED. FOR ONE THING, IT sounds so juvenile. I don't know anyone my age who gets grounded anymore. At least not that they talk about.

"That is so lame," says Abby when I call her on Sunday night, after my dad's gone, and tell her that I can't ride to school with her anymore. "What difference does it make *how* you get to school? I mean, as long as you go."

"I know. It's totally ridiculous. But when has life with my dad ever made sense?"

"And until school's out? Man, that totally sucks. You're going to miss some really good parties, Ruth."

Right, like my dad even lets me go to "really good parties" anyway. But I just say, "Yeah, I know."

"What happens after school's out?"

I force a laugh that is unconvincing. "My dad has it all figured out. I'll be working the counter at the tire store. Full time. And he's going to handle the money for me. Part of it will be used as my contribution to the household income, you know, since my mom doesn't work anymore. And the rest will be put into my college account. And, oh yeah, if there's any left over, and if I'm good, I will continue to get an allowance." I don't mention that I will be getting no allowance while I'm grounded—although I'm still expected to do the same chores. Well, the same plus Caleb's too.

"That's like slavery!" exclaims Abby.

"Tell me about it."

"Can't your mom do anything?"

Okay, I'm thinking Abby should know the answer to this by now. But in all fairness, her life is so totally different from mine that sometimes she just does *not* get it.

I try to explain that Mom is barely here. That she is the ghost mother, the green phantom, and I cannot expect one bit of support from her.

And finally there's a long pause. "Ruth?" she says in a serious voice. "How about, you know, the cutting thing?"

As much as I hate to lie to my best friend, I just cannot handle her getting on my case right now. "I'm fine," I tell her.

"Really?"

"Yeah. I can see how stupid that was. Really, I'm okay. Well, other than being totally frustrated about being grounded."

"Yeah. It seems really unfair. I just totally don't get your dad, Ruth."

"You and me both."

The next day I tell Glen about being grounded. He seems to understand this a little better than Abby.

"It's just the way those messed-up kind of guys think," he tells me as he walks me to the bus after school. "My dad was the same way. A real control freak. If Mom or I did anything he didn't approve of, man, you better watch out. We always felt like we were walking on eggshells when he was around."

"Yeah. That's exactly what it's like," I admit.

He looks at the big yellow buses lined up like kid-eating beasts, ready to devour the unfortunate losers who are forced to ride in their bellies. "I wish I could give you a ride home."

"Me too."

"You really think your dad would know?"

I shrug. "I don't honestly know how, but I wouldn't be surprised if he has spies watching me. Or maybe he'll take a break from work just to check on me." I squint down the street, looking for his ugly red truck amid the after-school traffic. "Who knows, he could be watching me even as we speak."

Glen nods. "That's like something my dad used to do. He even had this creepy set of field glasses hidden beneath the seat of his car."

"Right." My dad has binoculars too, and I think he does keep them in his pickup. So weird. "Anyway," I continue. "I think for at least the first day, I should just go along with it."

"Yeah." Glen gives me a little half smile. "Maybe things will lighten up later. My dad was like that. He'd blow up and lay down the law one day, and after a while, he'd sort of forget."

"Yeah, maybe." But even as I say this, I know this is where my dad and Glen's dad differ. Although Glen's dad was physically abusive, according to Glen, he was usually sorry afterward. But my dad, though verbally abusive, is never, ever sorry. And no matter what he does, he is always, always right. He is always justified, and the rest of us are stupid or rebellious or whatever adjective he's glommed onto for that day. And if anyone (at least in his immediate family) doesn't agree with him, he will blast them until they do. End of story.

***

A week passes, and I continue to comply with Dictator Dad's uncompromising rules. I can't really explain it, but it's like I've gone numb. I don't really care anymore. Nothing really matters. I've heard that people can endure a lot of pain if they're convinced there is an end in sight. Maybe that's the difference for me. That somehow, in the midst of all this, I think there is an end for me. And that in itself is comforting.

It's like when you're at the dentist and he tells you he's almost done, but he also tells you to let him know if you need any more anesthesia as he finishes his drilling. And even though it hurts, because you believe the end is in sight, you can actually put up with more drilling and pain than you could if you thought it was going to go on forever.

I think that's where I'm at right now. I have a feeling that the end is in sight. Like my pain doesn't have to last much longer. That I will soon be able to take control again. First I have to make it to the end of the school year. Don't ask me why. I just do. And then maybe I can end this thing. Stop the pain for good. Does this mean I'm going to cut too deeply one day? Perhaps. More likely, I'll just run away and live somewhere else. I'm not even sure what I'll do. But one way or another, I feel certain that, once and for all, I'm going to end this thing.

Unfortunately, Abby is getting really irritated at my lack of availability, not to mention the way I sort of check out a lot of the time. Maybe our friendship is on the line. But I can't do anything about it. I'm not sure I even care anymore.

"You're changing, Ruth," she tells me for like the hundredth time as we're walking to class. "It's like someone's done a lobotomy on you or something." She waves her hand in front of my face and then snaps her fingers. "Earth to Ruth. Come on, wake up, snap out of it."

I force a smile. "Sorry," I tell her. "Guess I'm just tired or something."

Glen is even concerned. "He's killing you, Ruth," he tells me this morning. "He's going to make you turn out just like your mom. Can't you see it?"

I just shrug. "What am I supposed to do?"

"Get help," he tells me.

"Help?" I just look at him, blankly I'm sure.

"Talk to a counselor or something."

"Like the *school* counselor?" I look at him like he's crazy. No one in their right mind would want to talk to Ms. Blanchard. Seriously, she looks like the biggest phony baloney of all time, like one of the Stepford wives.

"I don't know." I can tell he's discouraged, which makes me feel guilty. Like I'm raining on everyone's parade these days.

"I'm okay," I tell him. "And, hey, if it makes you feel better, maybe I will talk to Ms. Blanchard. I guess it couldn't hurt."

He brightens. "Yeah. I mean, it's free. And it's confidential. And who knows?"

"Yeah, who knows?" But even so, I'm certain that I will not talk to Ms. Blanchard. What good would it do?

"Besides, there's only one more week of school," he reminds me. "And this could be your last chance for a while. I mean to talk to Ms. Blanchard." And then he walks me down to the office to "help me" make an appointment. What is it with this guy? Is he like codependent or something?

Fortunately it's not too painful to make an appointment. You just tell the receptionist your name and who you'd like to talk to, and she gives you a little card with the time and date on it. No big deal. My appointment is scheduled for Monday morning at nine thirty. Great. I can hardly wait. Maybe I'll be sick that day.

Or sooner, as it turns out. The truth is, I've been cutting more than ever this past week. It's like I'm addicted, like I can't stop. As freaky as it sounds, and as much as I hate to admit it, it's almost like I've actually scheduled certain times to do it. I keep telling myself this is just a temporary thing, a quick fix that will eventually become unnecessary, because I do feel certain it will end as soon as the school year ends. My stress level will go down then and everything will change for the better. But for now I find myself cutting daily, sometimes three times a day. I usually cut just before lunch just so that I can make it through the rest of the day, and then again after I get home from school just to help me to relax, and almost always following any sort of "conversation" that I'm forced to endure with my dad.

And then today, just as I was experiencing a little relief right before lunch, things got messy. The last thing I remember, I was standing in the john, breathing deeply and trying to block out everything as I returned my little Altoids box to my pack. And then my ears began to buzz and I felt kind of lightheaded, then *wham!* The lights went out.

And now I am totally shocked to discover that I am lying on a couch in the health room. How did I even get here? I sit up and try to get my bearings, trying to remember what happened and listening to the conversation going on over by the doorway.

"Ruth is my best friend," I hear Abby pleading with someone. "Please, let me come in and see her."

"All right," says a woman's voice. "You might as well, since we've been unable to reach either of her parents."

"Ruth!" says Abby as she comes in and sits next to me. "Are you okay?"

I kind of shrug and look down at my hands, relieved to see that my sleeves are all the way down.

"What happened?" she demands.

It's coming back to me now, the bathroom, hitting my head . . . I reach up to feel a lump on my forehead. "I fainted," I tell her.

"Yeah, I know. Everyone's talking about it. Sherise Barrett heard you go down. She and a couple of her friends helped you down here."

"Yeah . . . I kind of remember now. I told her I was okay."

"Right." Now Abby puts her hand on my shoulder. "Were you doing it?"

"Doing it?" I say weakly.

"You know, cutting."

Now I firmly shake my head. "No. But I'm having my period, you know, and it's really bad this month. I think that's why I fainted."

"Oh." She sounds relieved.

So that's the story I tell the school nurse, and she buys it.

"I've left messages at your home and your dad's business," she tells me. "But no one has called back yet."

"That's okay," I assure her. "I'm fine now." I look at the clock and see that it's still lunchtime. "Can I go get something to eat? I think that's part of the problem, you know, like low blood sugar or something."

"Or maybe anemia," she says as she jots down a note. "But how's your head feeling?"

I reach up to touch it. "It's a little sore, but I think it's fine."

"Well, it's up to you whether you go back to class or not. I can't release you to go home until I speak to your parents, though."

I force a smile. "That's okay, really. I'll be fine. I just need to get something to eat."

"All right. I guess you can go. But if you start feeling bad, please, come back and see me."

"Sure," I tell her. "No problem."

But as Abby and I walk toward the cafeteria, I am more anxious than ever. That was close. Too close. Of course, all my friends are very concerned, and Glen asks if I'm okay, and while I should enjoy this attention, all I want to do is get out of here. I know they don't actually know that I'm a cutter—well, other than Abby, and even she's in her own little fantasy world of belief that I've quit—but I'm sure they could easily find out. Every comment they make reminds me of dogs sniffing around, trying to uncover something, or dig up an old bone that is buried somewhere. But I force a smile and offer evasive answers as I hurry to finish my lunch and leave.

"You sure you're okay, Ruth?" asks Glen as he joins me.

I try not to look too exasperated. "Yeah," I say. "I'm fine. I just fainted, okay? It was humiliating enough and I'd just like to forget it now. You know?"

He puts an arm around my shoulders as we walk down the hall. "Okay. I just happen to care about you. Is that a problem?"

I look up at him. "No," I tell him. "That's not a problem."

fourteen

It's Monday morning, and I find myself back in the office again. Only this time I'm not in the health room. This time I'm waiting in the counseling area. Glen politely escorted me down here, making certain that I keep my appointment to talk to the divine Ms. Blanchard of the perfect smile, whitened teeth, matching shoes and belts and handbags. Like she's going to understand someone like me. Yeah, right.

What am I even going to say to her? That my dad is mean? That he yells a lot? What can she do about that anyway? It's not like he's beating on us or anything. And he does work hard, he provides food and housing. Even if he is a disciplinarian, it's only because he cares about us? Right? Maybe I should just leave—

"Ruth Wallace?"

I look up to see her. Blonde hair perfectly in place, as usual, and, God help me, she is wearing a pale-pink sweater set and pearls! "Yeah?" I straighten out from the slumped position I had assumed while waiting.

"Come on into my office." Her voice is sugary sweet and makes me want to gag. She introduces herself, as if I didn't already know who she was. Give me a break.

"Sorry you had to wait." She smiles and holds the door open.

I slowly stand, pick up my bag, and follow her into her office. I think I'm literally dragging my heels. I so don't want to talk to this woman.

"Have a seat, Ruth." She takes a seat behind her neatly arranged desk, folds her hands in front of her, and then flashes that disgusting Colgate smile. "Let's talk."

I want to ask her what planet she's from and how she thinks she can possibly understand anything about me or my problems. But I simply sink into the chair and wait.

"How's it going?" she asks.

I shrug. "So-so."

"Hmm?" She gets a thoughtful expression now. "So-so? I suspect that means *not so well*?"

I shrug again. "Yeah, maybe."

Now she leans forward. "Do you want to tell me about it? Or do you want me to keep asking you questions?"

I shrug for a third time and consider telling her that this is all just a big mistake and that I should get to class now.

"Okay then, Ruth. You're the one who made this appointment. How about if you tell me what's bugging you. Okay?" Her smile's a little stiffer now, like she actually wants to get down to business.

Fine, why don't I just tell her? Why don't I just sit here and spill my guts and see if there's a single thing she can do about it? Which I seriously doubt, by the way.

And so I do. I tell her how mean my dad is. I tell her about how my mom had a breakdown last winter and how my brother couldn't take it anymore, how he ran away from home, but how it's just a matter of time before my dad figures it out and forces him to come back. I go on and on, not in an emotional way, but like I'm talking about someone else, like I'm describing somebody else's messed-up life. I don't mention cutting. What's the point?

"Wow," she says when I finally stop and lean back in my chair. "That's a heavy load. I'm surprised that you're holding up this well, Ruth." Then she studies me closely. "You've talked a lot about your family, but you haven't said much about how you're handling all this. How are *you* doing, Ruth?"

I sigh then shrug again. "I don't know."

"How do you feel when your dad yells at you?"

I don't say anything.

"How do you feel when you see your mom suffering? Do you miss how she used to be?"

"Of course."

"Do you miss your brother?"

"Yeah, I guess."

"How does that make you feel? How do you feel toward your dad about all this?"

"How do you think it makes me feel?" I snap. "How would you feel if you had to live like that?"

Now she doesn't answer, and I think I've probably got her stumped. I mean, seriously, what's she going to do? What can anyone do?

I pick up my bag and stand up. "I didn't figure there was anything you could do to help me," I say in a matter-of-fact voice. "I only came here because my friend wanted me to talk to someone. But thanks for your time anyway."

"Wait a minute, Ruth."

"Why?"

"Can you do something for me before you go?"

"What?"

She looks at me evenly and says, "Can you push up your sleeves for me, Ruth? On both arms?"

I just stare at her.

"Please?"

I glance at the door, ready to bolt. I wonder who told her about me? It must've been Abby. But how did Abby know that I was coming here today? I never mentioned it to her. Glen must've told Abby. But why? Why are my friends ganging up on me like this?

"Sit back down, Ruth," she says quietly.

I sit.

"Are you a cutter?" She is as calm and matter-of-fact as me.

"Who told you?" I demand, looking her straight in the eyes. "Was it Abby?"

She shakes her head. "No one told me anything, Ruth. I just guessed."

I'm feeling a little surprised here. I mean, this woman looks like a total airhead. How could she possibly guess about something like this?

"I know a little bit about cutting."

I'm sure my expression is skeptical, and she continues to explain.

"In fact, your story is familiar to me. Your dad sounds a lot like my dad. Only my dad didn't just yell. He hit us too."

I can tell by her face that what she's saying is true. And suddenly she looks like a real person to me, not a Stepford wife. Her eyes have a depth of sadness that I never noticed before.

"Really?" I say, falling into this. "Your dad was like that too?" *Then how did you turn out so freaking normal?*

"Yeah, it was pretty miserable."

"So . . . " I begin, unsure that I really want to go here. "Were you a cutter too?" She shakes her head. "No. But my younger sister was.

She was fourteen when I left home for college. She started cutting that same year."

"Oh."

"Yeah. I couldn't believe it when I figured it out. I was so sad. It's probably one of the main reasons I started to take psych classes and finally decided to major in counseling."

"Did your sister ever quit?"

"Yeah. But she had to get help, Ruth. She couldn't do it on her own. And back then, there wasn't much help to be found." Now Ms. Blanchard is smiling, and for the life of me I can't figure out why. "But things have changed, Ruth. There's help now."

"Help?"

"For cutters." She flips through a Rolodex then writes something down on a slip of paper. "My sister works at one of the few clinics that help cutters. It's called Promise House. I'm writing down the phone number for you." She hands me the paper. "Will you call her?"

"I . . . uh . . . I don't know. I mean, what does this involve? I'm sure it costs money . . . and there's no way I can tell my dad what I've been doing. He'd totally freak."

She nods. "Yeah. You're probably right. How about this? How about I call my sister and see what she recommends. Okay?"

"And you won't tell anyone else? I mean, like my parents—you won't call them and tell them about this, will you? Don't I have some kind of client confidentiality, or something like that?"

"Something like that. Although it's tricky, because you're still a juvenile. But trust me, okay?"

I can't see that I have much choice. Still, I'm not happy with this unexpected twist. I only came here today to see what I could do about my dad. He's the one with the big problem. And suddenly the focus has shifted to me. Like I'm the one to blame here. It just doesn't seem fair. But I play along and tell Ms. Blanchard that I trust her. She promises to get back to me in the next day or so.

"In the meantime, Ruth"—she looks right into my eyes now—"do you think you're in danger? I don't just mean from your dad. Are you safe from yourself? Do you think you can keep from cutting until I see you again?"

"Honestly?"

"Yes. Honestly."

I really consider this. "I don't know," I finally say. "And that's the truth."

She nods. "I understand."

To my amazement, I believe she does. Do I think that will make a difference? I honestly don't know. But I do feel a tiny flicker of hope, though hope itself kind of scares me these days. Every time I get hopeful, the rug gets pulled out from under me. And I'm just not sure how many more tumbles I can take.

fifteen

"How'd it go?" Glen asks me at the beginning of lunchtime, before I have a chance to slip off to the bathroom to cut.

"What?" I say dumbly, like I'm clueless as to what he's talking about.

"You know, Ruth, the counselor appointment."

I glance around to see if anyone's listening. It's not like I'm eager for everyone to hear that I went to the school counselor this morning, especially after my little fainting episode on Friday. They'll really think I'm a freak. I may be a mess, but I still have a little bit of pride. "Mind if we keep this private?" I say as we're heading into the cafeteria.

"Sure." He takes my hand now and gently pulls me out of the lunch line. "How about if we go out to lunch then? That would be private."

I consider this. If Dad sees me I'll be in even more trouble. On the other hand, what can he do to me? Ground me for life?

"Okay," I say, suddenly feeling like this could be fun. Maybe I need some fun. Maybe it's time I took some risks. What do I really have to lose anyway? "Why not?"

It feels so good to be sitting in Glen's car. Like maybe I'm still a real person and not just my daddy's robot girl. Maybe it's possible that I could have a life again. Maybe meeting with the counselor will change something. Or maybe I'll get better on my own. Or with Glen's help. Just being with him now kept me from cutting. Maybe that's a start.

"So, how'd it go?" he repeats as he leaves the school parking lot.

"Not as bad as I'd expected," I admit. "Ms. Blanchard is a lot nicer than I thought."

"Cool. Did she have any suggestions for how to deal with your dad?"

I'm not sure what to say now. "Sort of," I finally tell him. "She's going to get back to me in the next couple of days."

"That's great, Ruth. Maybe things are going to change."

"Yeah. Maybe." Of course, I'm not sure exactly how. Even if I can get into this Promise House place, there's no way my dad can remain in the dark. I'm sure he'll go through the roof when he hears what I've been doing to myself. It's not like I don't know that it's stupid and senseless and everything else I'm sure he'll say it is. I can only imagine all the new names he'll be calling me. I'm not sure I can take it.

"You don't sound too convinced." Glen pulls into a fifties-style drive-in restaurant, the kind where you get served in your car.

"Good idea," I say.

"Huh?"

"The drive-in," I tell him. "I'll feel safer about not being spotted if we stay in the car to eat."

"Yeah, that's what I was thinking."

"And do you mind if we don't talk about the whole counseling thing?" I make my best attempt at a smile for him. "I mean, it's been so long since I've had any kind of freedom. I'd like to just enjoy this. If you don't mind."

"No problem. And I totally understand how you feel. I just want you to know that I'm here for you, Ruth. If you need to talk."

"Thanks. And I really do appreciate that. But for right now I'd rather turn up the radio, chow down a burger, and pretend that life really is cool. Okay?"

"You got it."

So that's what we do. And it really does feel good to think that life could be like this. But even though it feels good, I know it's a deceiving kind of good. I know that reality will slug me in the gut again. Probably before the day is over. And it'll probably hurt even more coming on the heels of this moment.

I wonder if a person in prison ever feels like this. I mean, you could really torture prisoners by giving them a brief little taste of freedom and then slamming them back into their prison cell. Like, *Ha-ha, see what you don't get to enjoy?*

After school, I consider accepting Glen's offer of a ride. I already broke my dad's tyrannical manifesto at lunchtime. What's the big deal if I break it again? But then I decide not to risk it. Why push my luck?

"Thanks anyway," I tell him. "But I'd rather not take a chance."

"Well, you've only got a few more days of being grounded."

"Right." I look over toward the buses, which are already mostly loaded, and realize I better hurry. "See ya!"

At home, I go through my regular routine of chores, and I actually manage to function without cutting. I can see that my mom did a few things today, but they are kind of haphazard, like she didn't really put much effort into it. Even so, I tell myself it's better than nothing. I tell myself that it could be a beginning. It could be a turning point.

By five o'clock, I'm starting dinner. And I think that everything's under control, like I've done a good job and maybe this will be one of those rare nights when my dad doesn't lose it.

"Why didn't you put the garbage can out on the street this morning, Ruth?" he demands as soon as he has one foot in the door.

Monday, I'm thinking. This is Monday, trash pickup day, and I totally forgot to put the can on the street. Probably because I was freaking over my appointment with Ms. Blanchard. Now it'll be full for a whole week. Not just full but overflowing and stinking, and every time my dad sees it he will just get madder and madder.

"I'm sorry," I say, like that will change anything. "I totally forgot it was Monday."

"You're so stupid!" He throws his lunch box into the sink. "So worthless and stupid." Then he turns and glares at me. "How could you forget it was Monday?" He holds up his fingers. "First it's *Saturday* then *Sunday* and next comes Monday. Didn't you learn that in grade school, or maybe even kindergarten?"

"I just forgot—"

"What is it that's distracting you, Ruth? You been sneaking around with that boyfriend of yours?"

"No!"

"Well, what then?" he yells. "What is it that's distracting you?"

"I don't know." But I do know, and suddenly I'm freaking that he might know about my appointment with Ms. Blanchard. What if she called him and told him everything? Was I a fool to trust her?

"You're not only useless, Ruth, but you're completely hopeless as well!" Then he swears and heads off to the living room with his newspaper.

All things considered, it could've been worse. And although I tell myself this, I also feel like I'm at the end of my rope. I can't go on like this. The whole time that I'm fixing his dinner, I'm thinking about cutting. As I chop the lettuce for salad, I think about cutting. As I slice tomatoes, I think about cutting. As I chop onions, I think about cutting. And finally when dinner is finished and on the table, I have no appetite. All I want to do is go to the bathroom and cut. And that's exactly what I do. I don't even care that my dad is still in the house.

It isn't until Wednesday that I hear back from Ms. Blanchard. I get a note during first period and am excused to go to the office. Though I'm not sure that I totally trust her, I do feel fairly certain that she hasn't contacted my dad. I would've heard about it by now.

"Hi, Ruth," she says as I go into her office. "How's it going?"

I shrug. "About the same."

"Sorry I didn't get back to you sooner. But we were trying to get this set up."

"What? What are you setting up?"

"Okay, this is the plan: Nicole, that's my sister, she's got it all set for you to come to Promise House. She had to pull some strings, but because it was for me —"

"Wait," I say, holding up my hands. "Wait a minute. What does this mean? Who's going to pay for this? And what about my parents? What are you saying here?"

"Calm down, Ruth." She leans forward and gives me a fairly stern look. "Listen to me. Let me explain. Then you can ask questions. Okay?"

I take a deep breath and finally say, "Okay." But the truth is, I'm totally freaked. There's no way I can pull this off with my dad. I will be toast.

"Nicole has a spot for you. You will go as soon as school's out for the summer. On Saturday if you like. You'll stay there for thirty days —"

"Thirty days?" I practically shriek. "There's no way my dad will allow that. He has a job all lined up for me. He expects me to—"

"He *has* to allow you, Ruth. Trust me, he doesn't really have much of a choice. I've already written up a report. I've described the emotional abuse. I've made it clear that you are at risk and—"

"No. This is too much. You've gone too far. There's no way this is going to work. And what about my mom? And my brother?"

"Listen to me, Ruth. You can't rescue your mom or your brother. And you know you can't help your dad. All you can do is take care of yourself right now. And you have to stop cutting."

"I will. Really, I will. I can do this on my own. I don't need to be locked up in some clinic to get better—"

"Show me your arms, Ruth."

I look down at my lap, saying nothing.

"I mean it, Ruth. If what you're saying is true—if you can fix this thing yourself—then just show me your arms and prove it."

I still sit there silently as she gets up from her chair and comes around next to me.

"Show me your arms, Ruth. Prove to me you can handle this."

And so I unbutton the cuffs of my denim shirt and slowly push up my sleeves to reveal not just my old scars in various stages of healing, but all the many recent ones, including three new bandages.

"Oh, Ruth." Now she bends down and takes my hands in hers. "Look at me."

I reluctantly look up. "What?"

"You are going to beat this, Ruth. You are going to get well. But you can't do it on your own. Do you understand me? Your family is a big part of your problem, and you need to be someplace away from them. You need help to get well. Nicole and the other counselors know how to help. But you have to let them."

"But I—"

"No buts, Ruth. You know you have a problem. The first step toward healing is admitting that you have a problem. Can you do that?"

I look down at my horrible looking arms and nod my head. "Yeah, I guess so."

"Do you know that cutting is an addiction?"

I look back up at her, slightly confused, but also sort of getting it. "An addiction?"

"That's right. Like drugs or alcohol or gambling or sex or anorexia or whatever. It's an addiction. And it will take a lot of work on your part to get over it."

Somehow I know that she's right. Maybe not necessarily in my head, but somewhere inside of me, I do know she's right. "Okay," I finally say. "I'll do it."

She's got a pile of paperwork for me to read and sign. And feeling like I really have no choice, I give in and sign them.

"We'll handle your parents," she tells me. "The plan is to inform your father of what's going on when I pick you up."

"You pick me up?"

She smiles now. "Do you mind? I thought under the circumstances, well, maybe you could use a friend."

"Well, I, uh . . ."

"Is Saturday or Sunday better?"

I consider this. "My dad works until one on Saturdays. And he has Sundays off."

We decide that she'll come for me on Saturday at two. She will call my dad in advance and let him know that she needs to talk to him.

"What will you tell him?"

"Is your brother still gone?"

"Yeah."

"Well, I won't lie. But maybe I'll make him think it has to do with that."

"So he won't get mad at me?"

"Right. And I won't give him too much notice either."

"Thanks."

"You just have a bag packed and be ready to go."

"What if he says no?"

"He won't, Ruth. I'll have backup with me."

"Backup?" I imagine cops with guns.

She smiles. "Just a friend from Children's Protective Services. But he should be able to convince your dad that he has no choice in this matter."

"Do you think this will really work?"

She nods as she puts the paperwork back into a large yellow envelope. "I do."

I thank her and tell her that I hope she's right. However, I have my doubts. Just the same, I begin to formulate a plan.

sixteen

D AD INFORMS ME THAT I'M TO SHOW UP AT THE TIRE STORE FRIDAY AFTER
school to interview with the owner. When I ask why I have to meet
with the owner, he gets angry.

"I may run the place, but I don't own it, Ruth! Just because I
want to hire you doesn't mean that it's a sure thing. You have to
meet with Mr. Jackson and convince him that you'll be as good as I
told him." Then he laughs in a mean way. "Maybe you should wear
a skirt. Jackson's a leg man."

But I don't wear a skirt on Friday. I wear neatly pressed khakis
and my white linen shirt. I think I look fine. Besides, I'm hoping that
I'll never really have to work there. But there's no way I can tell my
dad that. To my surprise and relief, Dad actually agreed to let Abby
drive me over here.

"But then you stick around and ride home with me after work.
Might give you a chance to get to know some of the guys and see
how things work, so you don't make too much of a fool of yourself
if Jackson decides to hire you."

Mr. Jackson actually seems fairly nice. And I do my best to
convince him that I'm good on the computer and fairly friendly with
people, and when he asks about my GPA, he is finally convinced.

"Welcome to the Jackson's Tire Company team," he says. "Your dad says you'll be ready to start work on Monday."

I swallow and nod, wondering if he can see right through me. Does he know I'm lying? "Sounds fine."

But he just shakes my hand and then heads into one of the back offices. I nod to my dad to signal that I got the job, then I go sit in the waiting area. As I sit there, it occurs to me that I cannot stand the smell of tires. The acrid smell of rubber makes my eyes burn and my throat constrict. The prospect of working day in and day out in this brightly lit, stark atmosphere, where tacky posters of tires and wheels are plastered all over the place, makes me literally sick to my stomach.

"I heard you made the cut," says my dad when it's finally closing time and he's locking the front door.

"Yeah."

"Good. I was hoping that you wouldn't embarrass me too much."

I don't respond to that.

It's been a while since I've actually sat in my dad's pickup. But the way I feel now is exactly the same as when I was little. I don't want to do or say anything wrong. I think if I can be perfect and good that everything will be okay. Of course, I know better now. But I also know that it will do no good to rock my dad's boat. *Keep quiet and mind your manners.* That's what Mom used to tell us. Like that would make a difference.

Finally we're home and I go straight to the kitchen to start fixing dinner.

"Why don't we call out for pizza tonight?" says my dad.

I try not to look too shocked. "That sounds good." And he tells me what he wants on the pizza and to make the call. Feeling slightly off guard, I dial the phone and place the order. We haven't ordered pizza since before Mom's breakdown. I wonder what the special occasion is, then figure maybe it's me getting the job. Maybe Dad feels like his financial load is lightening now that I'll be contributing to the income. And I actually start to feel guilty. Like maybe I should forget about my little getaway plan, stick around, and help out like he expects me to. Be the good daughter.

Maybe I'll have no choice. I mean, Ms. Blanchard has her papers and her plans, but she hasn't met my dad yet. Somehow I think he could derail anyone. Even her.

My dad doesn't stick around for long after the pizza comes. He seems antsy, and I figure he must have someplace to go. For once he doesn't pick a fight with me to give him an excuse for going.

"Any plans tonight?" he asks me.

"Huh?"

"Well, it's the last day of school and you're not grounded now. I wanted to know if you had any plans."

I hear a trace of irritation in his voice. "Oh, I might call Abby. If that's all right."

"Just leave a note. Same as before." Then he takes off.

Feeling slightly stunned, I reach for the phone, dial Abby's cell number, and tell her the good news.

"Want to go to the party at the lake?" she asks.

"Oh, I'm not sure," I say, sure I'll end up getting caught at a party where alcohol will be flowing freely. My dad would probably ground me for the entire summer for being involved in something like that. "Maybe I better not."

"Why not? It's going to be fun."

"I just don't want to risk it with my dad. I'm barely out of hot water with him now. If anything went wrong . . . you know?"

"Yeah, I suppose you're right. I probably shouldn't go either, but

I already promised Phil Simmons that I would."

"You're going out with Phil?" The news registers like a surprise-party shout. Phil is a senior that Abby's had her eye on for months.

"Sort of. We've been talking some. Especially since my best friend has been so unavailable lately. I told him I'd go with him. But you could come with us—"

"No thanks." That totally settles it for me. No way would I horn into her first date with Phil. "But have fun, okay? And be careful."

She laughs. "Yeah. Don't worry. Hey, how did the job interview go?"

I tell her I got the job, but then add that it probably doesn't really matter.

"You mean because your dad is going to confiscate all your money anyway?"

I act like that's what I mean. But what I'd really like to tell her is that it's because I might be gone tomorrow. Still, I don't mention this. For one thing, I don't know for sure that it's really going to happen. And besides that, I'm not so sure I really want to go. I mean, what will this place be like? Then there's the fact that my dad was actually acting pretty civilized tonight. And I'm not even grounded anymore. Maybe things can change without me going off to some weird cutting clinic or whatever it is. I mean, I have no intention of cutting myself right now. Maybe I'm better already.

"Well, have a good night," says Abby finally.

"Yeah. You too."

About five minutes after I hang up the phone, it rings. To my pleased surprise, it's Glen.

"Abby said you're not grounded anymore."

"Did she call you?"

"Yeah."

"How pathetic is that?" I say. "Did she tell you that I was home alone on a Friday night?"

"Something like that. But I wasn't really wanting to go to the lake party either. I thought maybe we could hang together. That is, unless you'd rather stay home alone and wash your hair or watch reruns or something."

I laugh. "No, I'd love to hang with you. I need to go out to celebrate my new freedom."

So it's settled. He will pick me up in twenty minutes, just enough time for me to do a little primping and to change my clothes. I see my mom, the green phantom, slipping down the hallway as I come from the bathroom, and I'm tempted to say something to her. But just like that she's gone. The bedroom door closes silently.

Then Glen is here and we're off to see what kind of fun we can dig up on a Friday night. The town feels full of life as Glen drives down Main Street. It's balmy and warm, and for the first time in a long time, I'm feeling really alive and hopeful.

"I think things are changing," I say to Glen. "I got a job and my dad's acting nicer, and I think maybe it's going to get better."

He smiles, but I can see a trace of concern in his smile. "I sure hope so, Ruth. For your sake."

We finally decide to go to a movie and get there just as it's beginning. As a result we have to sit in the front row, and because it's an action adventure flick, I start to feel like I'm actually participating in the film. But it's a good distraction. Otherwise I'm sure I would be obsessing about tomorrow. I have no idea which way this thing is headed. I'm not even sure which way I want it to go. Finally the movie is over and we're back outside.

"That was pretty good," I tell him as we walk back to his car. "Thanks!"

"Sorry about the seats," he says.

I just laugh. "Hey, it added to the excitement."

We go out for coffee again, just like we did on our first date, and I'm really tempted to tell Glen all about Ms. Blanchard's plan for me. But that would mean revealing my little problem. And I'm not ready for that. In fact, I'm not sure I will ever be ready for that. Besides, I'm telling myself, I think I'm over it now. I think I've got the upper hand in this. I honestly don't think I'll ever need to cut again. Why should I, if life keeps going like this? I'm not grounded. My dad will respect me because I have a job and am contributing. And there's Glen. How much better can things get?

Even so, I tell Glen that I should get home by eleven. And just as I say this, it occurs to me that I totally forgot to write my dad a note. Oh, crap! I feel like someone just dumped a bucket of ice water over my head. If Dad gets home before me, I will be in serious trouble.

"What's wrong?" asks Glen as we walk outside.

"Oh, nothing."

He reaches for my hand. "Come on, Ruth. I know something's wrong. You've got the worst look on your face. What's up? Did I say something—"

"No. It's not you." I turn and look at him. His face, lit by the overhead streetlight, shows his concern. "You're great, Glen. It's really nothing you did. I just realized that I forgot to leave my dad a note before I left. So I'm just hoping he's not home yet." I take in a deep breath. "Chances are, he isn't. I mean it's a Friday. He's probably at The Dark Horse, putting away another beer even as we speak."

Glen nods then moves his face closer to mine. "Yeah, I bet that's what he's doing." And then, right there on the sidewalk, he leans down and kisses me. I'm so surprised and amazed. It's like the sweetest, best feeling I can imagine. Then I kiss him back. And we kiss for a few seconds. And, man, it is so good.

He stops suddenly. "Just in case, Ruth, I should get you home right away. I mean, I don't want you getting grounded again after just one night of freedom."

But it's funny. After kissing Glen, I don't feel nearly so worried about my dad. I have no idea why this is, but even when I see my dad's pickup in the driveway, I don't totally freak.

"Hope it goes okay," says Glen. "You probably don't want me to walk you to the door, right?"

"Yeah. That'd probably be better. Thanks for everything. It was great."

"See ya," he calls as I get out.

Now I'm heading up the walk toward our house, telling myself to just chill. Everything's going to be fine. I've got a job and Dad was in a good mood tonight. Things are changing. Also, the lights are on. That's a good sign. But as soon as I'm inside, I know that I'm in for it.

"Where have you been?" he booms at me before I can even close the door.

"I'm sorry. I totally forgot to leave a note. It's just that Glen called and—"

"I can't believe you, Ruth! You're barely out of trouble and the next thing I know you're running out of here half-cocked and you screw up all over again. What is wrong with you?"

"I'm sorry, I just—"

"I don't want your worthless apology, Ruth! I want you to obey my rules. I want you to respect me. I want you to use your head! Things have got to change around here! I'm sick and tired of the crap I get from you kids, from your mom. This whole family makes me want to . . . "

But I'm tuning it out now. As best I can anyway. The words are so familiar that I know them by heart. The rhythm, the beat of his speech. I think I could do it in my sleep. Then he uses the word that cuts deep. He calls me "half-breed" a few times, and he probably sees me flinch and consequently thinks he's gotten my attention.

"I don't know why I even try," he's saying now. "You guys are all just a bunch of losers." Now he leans down and looks at me, and to my surprise he seems almost sad. "I was starting to have some hope for you, Ruth. I thought getting a job would help you to grow up and take on some more grown-up responsibilities. But you just keep letting me down. Again and again. I guess that's all I should expect from a half-breed." Then he turns and walks away. And it's weird, I think I would prefer being yelled at. This other thing, a guilt trip or whatever you want to call it, actually hurts even more than just plain yelling and swearing.

And as I go to the bathroom, I'm thinking he's probably right. I probably am a loser. I mean look at me. Here I am hiding out in the bathroom, sneaking out my precious razor blade, and slicing into my own flesh. What kind of a freak really lives like this?

seventeen

AFTER I'M DONE, AFTER I'VE BANDAGED MY ARM, AFTER I'VE EXPERIENCED A brief form of relief, I am sorry. Not so much for the actual cut. I'm used to that. But I'm sorry that I couldn't control myself, couldn't keep myself from doing what I didn't want to do. I'd been telling myself all day that I don't really need help, that I can stop this thing myself. And then, during my date with Glen, I was actually convinced that I didn't need to go to some stupid clinic for cutters. I was ready to tell Ms. Blanchard, "Thanks, but no thanks. I can handle this myself." Now I'm not so sure.

It doesn't help anything to know what I'll be losing if I do decide to go. First of all, there's Glen. It's like that relationship I really, really want is just starting to happen. And now I have to go off and leave him for a whole month? During the summertime? There's no way he'll wait that long for me. Especially when he finds out why I'm gone. And how do I keep that a secret? I'm sure Abby will figure it out. Abby. I'll miss her too. Our friendship is already in a rocky place. When she finds out that I never really quit cutting, what then?

Then there's the job. Not that I want it. I really hate the idea of working in the tire store, being under my dad's ever-watchful eye. But I wouldn't have minded earning some money, taking some of the stress off my family.

And what about Caleb and my mom? What will happen to them? All these worries pile up on me like a bunch of heavy stones until it seems I can barely breathe. Until I feel certain that I must stay home. How can I possibly leave?

Even so, I follow Ms. Blanchard's instructions and pack a bag—just in case. And then I go to bed and try to sleep, but I think it's about three in the morning before I actually do.

When I wake up, it's almost ten thirty. I'm glad my dad's not around to see how late I slept. I can just hear him saying that I'm a lazy, good-for-nothing half-breed as I crawl out of bed and head for the bathroom. It's amazing really, the way his words echo inside of me even when he's not around.

I shower and dress and go through the paces of my chores without really thinking. I feel like a robot, like my dad has programmed me and this is the only way I can actually operate. I remind myself of how stupid I am when I take the trash out to the garage. Our can is packed full, and I've had to put the additional trash in a plastic bag that keeps falling over and spilling. I don't know how many times I've picked up bits and pieces of garbage from the garage floor. All this because I forgot to put the can on the street last week. I really am pathetic!

Even so, I manage to have all my chores done by one o'clock. Knowing my dad will be home any minute, I go to my room and just wait. I don't want to have to talk to him before Ms. Blanchard arrives.

It's weird, but I'm actually getting worried that she might not come at all. I'm thinking that maybe I got my facts wrong, that maybe I even imagined this whole thing. And the possibility that I really do want her to come is downright freaky. Maybe I really do want to get out of here. Then I consider my mom. If I really am leaving, maybe I should go tell her good-bye. Or would that just upset her? Or would she even care?

So I tiptoe down the hallway, knock on her door, wait a few seconds, and then go in. As usual, she's in her green bathrobe, sitting in her rocker, bright afghan in her lap, vacant look across her face.

"Mom?" I move closer, unsure whether she even knows I'm in here. Then she looks up and almost smiles. Or maybe it's her eyes that are almost smiling, because her mouth is a straight line. Or maybe it's just a glimmer of recognition, like she really does remember me after all.

"I just wanted to talk to you," I tell her.

To my surprise she reaches out and takes my hand. This gesture alone almost makes me cry. Almost. But she doesn't say anything.

"I just wanted to tell you I love you," I say in a slightly shaky voice. "And no matter what happens, I will always love you. And I hope you get better soon. I hope we all get better soon."

She sort of nods now. And her eyes are shiny, like she's about to cry too. But she doesn't. Neither of us shed a single tear. We just sit there until I hear a door opening in the house, followed by heavy footsteps that belong to my dad. I can tell by her eyes that she hears them too.

Then I lean down and hug her and quickly leave. Slipping back into my room, I hole up there and listen to my dad moving through the kitchen. I know exactly what he's doing. He goes through the mail, sets the newspaper aside, then checks to see if I've done my chores, including whether I've made him some lunch. Fortunately I have. It's just another tuna-fish sandwich, but I'm sure he'll eat it.

I hear the squeak of the kitchen chair as he settles down with his lunch and newspaper. And I wonder if Ms. Blanchard has contacted him like she said she would. I wonder if she is coming at all.

Despite my longing to stay here and make myself stop cutting and keep dating Glen and everything, I am suddenly sure I will fall completely apart if Ms. Blanchard does not show. I'm hanging onto this last tiny thread, and if it breaks . . . well, I just don't know.

I hear the doorbell. I get up and open my bedroom door just slightly, enough so that I can hear who is there. I can tell by the sweet ringing voice that it is Ms. Blanchard. And I can tell that Dad is taking her into the living room and she is doing most of the talking. I can't quite discern the words, but I know she's explaining something. And then I hear my dad calling me. "Ruth!" he yells for the second time. "Come out here."

Feeling like a trapped mouse, I go out and stand in the doorway between the hall and the living room.

"Hi, Ruth," says Ms. Blanchard with a smile. She is wearing a soft yellow shirt and white pants with coordinating accessories. Her purse and shoes match.

"What's this she's saying about you, Ruth?" asks my dad, using his controlled voice as if he were talking to an irate customer. "Ms. Blanchard says that she's taking you somewhere, that you have a problem. What's this about, Ruth?"

I look at Ms. Blanchard, hoping she'll handle this, give me some kind of clue, or better yet, just take over.

"Ruth needs to go away for treatment," she says calmly, as if this is something that happens every day. "I'm taking her to a place where she can get the help she needs." She nods to the packet of papers sitting on his lap. "I need you to sign the forms where they're marked with those yellow tabs." She looks back at me. "You go get your things, Ruth. I'll finish explaining the legalities to your dad."

The way she says *legalities* seems to give her the upper hand, and so I go back to my room and add a few more things to my bag.

I think maybe I really am ready to leave.

"Well, I'll sign these," my dad is saying. "And you can take her today. But I'm calling an attorney and I'll have her back here by Monday. You can count on that."

"Do what you think you need to do," she tells him.

"And don't you be thinking I'm paying for any of this nonsense." He holds the pen in his fist like a weapon. "Because I'm not forking over one cent for the state's stupidity."

"It's all been taken care of," she assures him.

I hover in the hallway, waiting for him to finish signing the papers. I have no idea what she said to him while I was in my room. But apparently he has agreed to this. At least for now. I'm guessing she mentioned something about Caleb and the protective-services people. I suspect she has my dad cornered, and he knows he doesn't have a leg to stand on, at least for the moment.

He's scowling when I come out. "I don't know what kind of nonsense you think you're pulling now, Ruth, but you can be sure I'll get to the bottom of it."

"Feel free to call the caseworker," says Ms. Blanchard. "Her number is on that card I just gave you. She can answer any of your questions. Or your attorney's." Then she turns to me. "Ready, Ruth?"

For the first time that I can remember, my dad is perfectly speechless. His mouth is partially open, but he's just standing there with some papers still in his hand, saying nothing. But, oh, is he ever mad. I can see it in his eyes. Like a smoldering volcano, he is ready to blow.

"Let's go," says Ms. Blanchard, and I wonder if she feels it too.

There are two cars in the driveway. And I remember how she said she'd be bringing backup. She hands the packet of papers to the man in the other car, and we get into her car, and finally we are pulling away from my house. I think I can breathe again.

"I'm worried about my mom," I say suddenly.

"Is she home?"

"Yeah. She's always home." It hits me full force now. "And now that Caleb and I are gone, I'm worried . . . what if he takes it out on her?"

"Do you think he'd hit her?"

"I don't know. He'll yell at her at least. And that can be just as upsetting, you know."

"I know." She considers this. "Is there anyone you can call? A family member or friend who can check up on her."

"Her brother," I say suddenly. "I'll bet Uncle Rod could help her."

Ms. Blanchard hands me her cell phone and before long I am talking to my uncle. I explain that I am leaving home for about a month and that I'm worried about my mom. I manage to do this without actually mentioning exactly why it is that I have to go. And, to my relief, he doesn't ask.

"Don't worry, Ruth. I'll check on her. Maybe I can even talk her into leaving now. Now that you kids are gone, she doesn't have any reason to stay."

"That's true," I say with realization. "She really doesn't. Maybe this can be her ticket out too."

"I sure hope so."

And so I feel a little relief as Ms. Blanchard drives me down the highway. "Where are we going?" I ask.

"Promise House is a couple of hours from here. About twenty minutes from Crawford, kind of out of the way."

"That sounds out of the way." Now I'm feeling a little worried. "Is it the kind of place where you're locked up?"

She laughs. "No. Trust me, I think you're going to like it."

I want to trust her. So far she hasn't given me any reason not to. But at the same time I feel this blanket of sadness covering me. Like, how pathetic am I that I have to be transported to some nuthouse where people are treated for hurting themselves? Really, how sad is that?

But I keep these thoughts to myself. I just stare out the window and watch the countryside pass by. I watch cows in a pasture and wish my life were as simple as theirs. Just eat your grass, drink your water, soak up the sun, and sleep whenever you like. Oh, sure, they're destined to become hamburger or somebody's new shoes, but they don't know that. Maybe ignorance really is bliss.

Don't think about anything. Just chill and see what happens next. And, hey, if this place doesn't work out, I can just leave. Right? But where will I go?

Don't think about anything.

eighteen

Ms. Blanchard turns down a long driveway that leads to what looks like an old farmhouse and several outbuildings. But it's not run-down at all. In fact, everything appears to be in good shape, like someone actually cares, and there's a big wraparound porch, where several girls are sitting on the steps.

She parks off to the side and I get out, pull out my bag and backpack, and slowly walk with her up to the porch. Why is this so hard? As I get closer I can see that the girls on the porch are smoking. And for some reason this surprises me. Not that I've never seen anyone smoke. I mean, Caleb does and a few of my friends do. Even my dad does, although he likes to pretend he doesn't. But I guess because I sort of assumed this was a clinical kind of place, I never figured that smoking would be allowed.

"Hey," says a girl with short red hair before she takes a long drag. "Welcome to the nuthouse."

I glance nervously at Ms. Blanchard, and she just smiles. "Hi, girls. This is Ruth. Your new enlistee."

"Lucky you," says an overweight girl. She has bad acne and is wearing a black knit cap pulled low on her forehead, a strange fashion statement for such a warm June day. "Hope you enjoy your stay."

We go inside and I am introduced to a woman named Juanita,

who asks me to fill out some paperwork, forms that seem mostly medical in nature. I do the best I can but can't really remember when I had my last tetanus shot, although I think it was in sixth grade when I stepped on a nail. And what childhood diseases have I survived? At the moment it seems somewhat miraculous that I've survived at all. I look around hopelessly, wishing someone would give me a clue here, but Ms. Blanchard has gone off in search of her sister.

After I finish the forms, I receive a three-page questionnaire. "You can fill this out later if you want," Juanita tells me. "No big hurry, but sometime today would be good."

"Right." I glance around the foyer where I've been sitting. The house seems clean and well maintained but somewhat sparse.

"There she is," says Ms. Blanchard as she comes down the stairs with a tall, dark-haired woman. "Ruth, this is my sister, Nicole."

Nicole holds out her hand to shake mine. "Nice to meet you, Ruth."

"Nice to meet you too," I stupidly echo.

"I'm sure you feel pretty weird right now," says Nicole. "But that's how everyone feels when they first arrive. Don't worry, it'll get better in time."

"I have to get going now," says Ms. Blanchard as she puts the strap of her purse over her shoulder. "But I know you're in good hands, Ruth. These people know what they're doing."

I nod, but I am sorry to see her go. She seems like my last connection to my old life. "Thanks," I mutter. "Have a good drive back."

Nicole gives me a quick tour of the house, which is mostly bedrooms, a meeting room, a kitchen, and a dining room. "Everyone helps out," she says, pointing to a job roster on the bulletin board. "We try to be like a real family."

A real family? What is that? Like on TV? Like the Osbournes? They're real, aren't they? And in some ways not so different from my own.

"I know this is hard," Nicole is telling me. "And it'll continue to be hard for a while. But if you let us, we can help you. You just have to be open."

The smoker girls are coming back inside now. Nicole calls to one of them. "Alexi," she says. "Can you come here?"

The overweight girl with the ski cap joins us. "What?"

"Ruth is your new roommate," Nicole tells her. "Can you take her to her room and show her where to put things?"

Alexi doesn't look too thrilled with this assignment but says, "Yeah, I guess."

"Thank you."

So I follow this girl up the stairs and down a hall until we get to room 4B. "This is it," says Alexi. "You get the bed by the window. I would've taken it but I have asthma."

I want to ask her why she's smoking if she has asthma, but I know to keep my mouth shut.

"This is your closet," she says, pointing to a narrow closet on my side of the room. "Spacious, I know, but most of us travel light." She looks at my bag. "Looks like you do too."

I set my bag on the bed and look around. The room, like the rest of the place, is fairly sparse. Two twin beds, two bedside tables with reading lamps, a wooden chair by each bed, and other than a poster on the wall between the two beds, that's pretty much it. I look up at the poster, which is only words. "By his stripes you are healed." I have no idea what that means. Like is it talking about some magical zebra or tiger? Again, I don't ask. Maybe I don't want to know.

"Our bathroom is down here," continues Alexi as she leads me to the end of the hall. "We share it with four other girls." The larger-than-average bathroom is neat and clean. There are two toilets in stalls, so at least I can expect some privacy. Alexi is standing near the sinks, holding up her hand gracefully, like she's a game-show girl showing off the prizes. She points to a shelf that's divided into six portions. "*This* is your part of the shelf," she says dramatically, "to hold your *personal* items."

"Right."

"And," she says, "I guess that's about it. Any questions?"

I shake my head.

"Then I shall depart."

"Thanks," I say in a mousy voice. I go back to my room and unpack my bag. I'm not even sure why; it just seems the right thing to do. I hang my shirts on the wire hangers and then set my folded jeans and things on the shelves at the bottom of the closet. Since there's no dresser, I assume that's what the shelves are for. Then I take my "personal items" and put them on the shelf in the bathroom. Now I'm not sure what to do. It's not quite five o'clock, and dinner's not until six. I remember the questionnaire I'm supposed to fill out "sometime today" and figure that might be a good way to waste an hour.

The questions are really hard. Not hard like a test I forgot to study for, but hard as in I'm not sure I want to write down honest answers, or any answers at all for that matter. And some of the questions seem pretty subjective, like I could write down any answer and not be right or wrong. Finally, I just decide to get it over with. It's not like I'm going to be graded, right? And maybe I don't even know what the truth is anyway. Isn't that why I'm here? So they can straighten me out?

I meet the rest of the girls at dinner. I'm guessing there are about thirty or so all together. But there's no way I can remember all their names. I do get that the redhead who was smoking on the porch is Charisa, and she seems to be some sort of leader here—or at least most of the girls seem to respect her.

I'm kind of surprised when Nicole says a prayer before the meal is served. I didn't realize this was a religious kind of place. But it's only a short prayer, a thanking-God-for-the-food sort of thing. We sit at two long tables that pretty much fill this room. Several girls who are on KP today bring us serving dishes of food. Everyone has KP one day a week, and they're expected to work on all three meals for that day. Nicole said that I'll be on the chores roster starting Monday.

"Sunday is kind of a day off for everyone," she explained earlier. "We have meetings, but that's about it. There aren't chores to speak of, other than making your bed. And no classes. You pretty much just get to hang out. It's a good time to get to know the other girls."

I'm not so sure I want to get to know these girls. I can already tell that some of them are pretty messed up. Like my roommate, for instance. After having a closer look, I now know why she wears that ugly ski cap. It's because she's bald. What's up with that? And then this chick sitting next to me, she's got on a sleeveless top and her arms are a mess from cutting. They're also covered with these small round scars, which I'm guessing are cigarette burns. Gross! I can't believe she doesn't want to cover it up. It almost made me lose my appetite.

As dinner winds down, some of the girls start to argue about which DVD they're going to pick for "movie night." I swear a couple of them look like they're about to get into a catfight over it. Maybe this place really is a nuthouse.

Finally, it's time to clear the tables. I follow the example of the other girls, scraping my plate into a plastic trough, then depositing my dishes and utensils in the designated places. Then I sort of slip out the door, go upstairs, and take refuge in my room. Rather, *my side* of the room.

Okay, I feel really frustrated now. I don't know exactly why. I mean, no one's said or done anything to hurt my feelings, but I feel so displaced, so lost, and even a little lonely. Do I wish I were home getting yelled at by my dad right now? Maybe so. At least I know the rules to that game. But here, I'm locked up with a bunch of crazies, and who knows what might happen next? It's really pretty freaky.

Even though it's only seven o'clock, I feel like going to bed now. I wonder if anyone would notice, or even care.

But then I would feel so stupid if they came up here, looking for me, and saw that I was in bed. Maybe they have rules about that. I know I signed an agreement to abide by the rules, but I was so nervous that I read the list pretty fast. And now I can't even remember what the rules are. I try to take deep breaths, try to relax, but it's like I just keep feeling more and more uptight. And then it occurs to me that my old faithful Altoids box is still in my backpack.

Okay, I do remember that one of the forms I filled out asked whether I had brought anything sharp or dangerous with me, and naturally I checked no. It's not like I had actually forgotten about the Altoids, but I figured I could always say that in my defense. That little red-and-white tin seems to be calling to me now, promising me some relief, a little bit of peace and comfort.

But I can still hear girls moving around the house like they haven't started the movie yet. Some are coming upstairs, and I can hear some of them using the bathroom, and I wonder where I can possibly do this. Where is a place that's private?

I decide that I must simply wait until things quiet down. Movie time begins at eight, and I expect that most of the girls will be downstairs by then. If I can just keep it together for fifty-five minutes, then everything will be okay.

And so I wait. When Alexi comes in to get something, I pretend to be working on that questionnaire. Like I'm trying to do a really good job.

"You coming to see the movie?" she asks as she rummages through a paper bag in her closet. She finally emerges with several candy bars, which she quickly pockets. I can tell she didn't want me to see that, so I pretend not to notice.

"I don't think so," I tell her. "I'm kind of tired. It's been a long day, you know."

"Yeah, it's always like that at the beginning."

The beginning of what? I just nod like I know what she means then turn back to my questionnaire.

Finally the upstairs is quiet, and I'm pretty sure the movie is starting by now. It's a little after eight when I creep down the hall to the bathroom, Altoids box in the back pocket of my jeans. I go into the stall farthest from the door, put the lid down on the toilet, and sit. I hold my breath for a few seconds, just to listen and make sure no one's coming upstairs. But it's still quiet.

Within minutes I am done with my little deed. I hold a wad of toilet paper against the cut, pressing it hard to stop the bleeding. But I totally forgot about bandages. They're still in my backpack. I listen carefully before I emerge from the stall, still holding the toilet paper to my arm, making sure that no one's around. Then I even snoop through the other girls' shelves to see if anyone else has some bandages that I could "borrow." Of course, there are none. What am I thinking?

So, keeping the wad tight against my arm, I pull down my sleeve and tiptoe back to my room. I quickly locate my box of Band-Aids. Then, with my clothes still on, I get into bed and pretend to sleep.

But as I lie here with my eyes closed, all I can think is that I am a stupid mess. A big stupid mess. And I don't see how anyone can ever straighten me out.

nineteen

SOMEHOW I MAKE IT THROUGH SUNDAY WITHOUT CUTTING. OH, I GET TEMPTED, all right, especially when my roommate is anywhere nearby. I have really tried to avoid her today. I don't know what it is about Alexi—and believe me, it could be lots of things—but it's like I cannot stand this girl. I can't stand to see her, or hear her, or even smell her. And it's not just because she's fat, but it's like how she talks in this sort of dramatic, sarcastic way—like she's the star of the show, and everything is all about her.

On top of everything else, she farts in bed. Really loud, like she gets a kick out of it. Talk about sick! Even my brother, Caleb, isn't that gross. And she snores—I mean seriously snores. I think I was awake half the night listening to her sawing logs. Just the thought of this girl makes me want to cut myself!

So I'm wondering, how am I supposed to get better at this place if my roommate makes me want to cut? Even so, I keep telling myself that I won't give in to this. If I can resist the urge to cut today, I might be able to make a better case of getting out of here sooner. Which is what I think I want to do. I want out of here ASAP. I plan to speak to Nicole about it first thing Monday.

Then Monday is here and suddenly I'm going to classes and group sessions and doing chores and doing my journal assignments, and there's no chance to tell Nicole that I want out. So I end up in the bathroom stall with my trusty Altoids box, and I tell myself that I can give this place another day.

Tuesday comes, and I sit through the classes and group sessions, doing my time, and I do my chores and journal assignments. I say as little as possible to everyone, and finally it's time for bed, and I'm actually pretty tired. Amazingly, I have *not* cut myself.

Then Wednesday comes and I am totally fed up. I'm sick and tired of hearing these girls going on and on about their stupid lives during group sessions. Okay, I realize that some of them have really big problems. Some have been sexually or physically abused, and it's no surprise that they're cutters. And then you have girls like Jessica, who's been cutting herself since her dog died. *Her dog died*—give me a break! And then you have the freaking crazy ones like my room-mate. She's not only a cutter but she pulls her hair out too. That's why she's bald. She's even pulled out her eyebrows and eyelashes. She says she does it because she's fat. Like being bald makes it easier to be fat? What*ever.*

"So you think you're better than the rest of us, Ruth?" demands Charisa at this afternoon's group session.

"Huh?" I snap to attention, since I'm pretty sure she's talking to me. "What?"

"I *said,* do you sit there while we talk just thinking you're so much better than us?"

"No," I stammer. "I never said that."

"Sure, you never *said* it. But we can tell just by looking at you that it's what you're thinking. Right, guys?"

Everyone pretty much nods. I'm not sure if it's because it's Charisa making this accusation or what, but I have no idea how to respond. I've been in this same small group for three days now and

I know most of the names of the other seven girls, as well as their problems. I guess I'm just a little tired of all their whining.

"Is that true?" asks Nicole, our moderator.

"What?" I say, stalling for time.

"Do you think you're better than the other girls?"

"No." I shake my head and look down at my lap.

"You do too," snaps Charisa. "Everyone can see it."

"That's right," says Alexi. "You're always looking down your nose at me. You think I can't tell?"

Well, that just does it. Something in me can't take it. "Okay!" I say loudly. "Maybe it's true. Maybe I don't think I need to be here. So what?"

Alexi just laughs now. "Yeah, talk about denial. Ruth Wallace wins the cake. We should call her Cleopatra, cuz she be da queen of de Nile." Then she does this cheezy Egyptian thing like she's the first person who ever thought of that ancient joke, and everyone laughs.

I totally snap. I want to hit Alexi. I want to smash her ugly face in. I stand up and point at her. "Look, I'm not like you, okay? I'm not messed up like you are. I mean, look at yourself! You're a one-woman freak show. And I have to share a room with you. I have to listen to you snoring like a stupid buzz saw every night. And I have to smell your freaking farts! And I have to—" Suddenly I feel sick and shocked, like I cannot believe I have just said that. What is wrong with me?

I can tell by her face that I hurt her. But she's right back at me now. "And you think you're little Miss Perfect? You think you can pull something over the rest of us? We know you're just as messed up as the rest of us. Only you're never going to get better, little Miss Perfect, because you can't even admit it."

"Admit what?" I no longer care what she or anyone else in this room thinks.

"That you can't quit cutting yourself. Yeah, you sit there one meeting after the next, you listen to the rest of us telling about our problems, but you can't even admit that you're a cutter. And I happen to know that you've been cutting yourself since you got here too."

Now the room gets quiet. And I know this is considered a serious offense. Cutting is definitely against the rules.

"Is that true?" asks Nicole.

I don't answer. I just stare at Alexi like I wish she were dead. And I do. I really wish she were dead.

"It's true," spits Alexi.

Nicole and everyone else are looking at me now.

"Ruth?" says Nicole in a calm voice. "Have you been cutting?"

"No." I look down at the floor now.

"Liar!" says Alexi.

I don't respond.

"Ruth, we'll talk privately after the session," says Nicole.

And then she continues with the session. I just sit there like a stone. All I can think is that I want out of here. Let me out of the loony bin before I really hurt someone.

Nicole leads me to her office after the session ends. "Have a seat," she says then sits across from me.

"Why did you let Alexi treat me like that?" I say.

"You both said some ugly things, Ruth."

"But she started it." I guess I'm hoping that if we can keep this focused on Alexi, I might somehow escape.

"That's what happens sometimes. The girls won't tolerate having someone in their group who won't participate."

"I participate."

"No, Ruth. You pretend to participate. But you're not really sharing. Don't feel bad, though. A lot of girls start out the same way. Good grief, it took Alexi two weeks before she finally gave in."

I consider this. "But what I said was true. I can't stand Alexi. I hate being her roommate. She makes me totally sick."

"You were sick before you got here, Ruth. Alexi might bring the sickness to the surface. But that might be a good thing too."

"A *good thing*?" I hear the volume of my voice increasing. "How can it be a good thing if she makes me want to cut?"

Nicole nods. "So Alexi was telling the truth."

I don't say anything.

"Have you been cutting, Ruth?"

"I want to go home," I say. "I can't stand this place. I can't stand Alexi."

"Well, at least you're being somewhat honest now, Ruth. That's progress. But you still need to answer my question. Have you been cutting?"

"A little."

"Show me your arms."

I feel a mixture of shame and anger as I push up my sleeves. But there's another part of me that doesn't even care.

She examines my newest cuts. "What are you using to cut with?"

"Razor blade."

"Did you bring it with you?"

I nod.

"This means Juanita will have to go through all your things now."

I sort of remember this from one of the forms I signed. It was a trust agreement. I had broken it, which gives them the right to do random searches now. It's like I've been demoted a security level.

"I really want to go home," I tell her again. "I don't think this place is helping me. I think I'd do better on my own."

She smiles. "I wish I had a dollar for every time I've heard that. I could probably retire tomorrow."

"I mean it," I say.

"I'm sure you do. But without treatment and commitment, those are just empty words. You might as well be a drug addict who says she won't use again, or an alcoholic who promises not to drink. This is the truth: You will not get over this without help, Ruth. But you *can* get over it. First of all, you have to be willing. You have to want to get well."

"I *do* want to get well. Why do you think I agreed to come?"

"Good. And you've come to the right place, and we want to help you. But you're the only one who can make it happen. You have to cooperate with the program. You have to participate with the groups. You have to be honest, Ruth. You have to accept that you have a serious problem. You have to be willing to examine the reasons why you started cutting. And then you have to deal with them."

"But it's so hard."

"Would it be easier to keep on cutting?"

I don't answer.

"I know how it feels, Ruth. I've been there. Cutting rules your life. It keeps you on the outside of things. You feel like an outcast. You think it's a way to deal with your pain, but it only brings a different kind of pain." She pauses. "And then you have to hide it from your friends. You keep lying to yourself, thinking you're going to quit, but you can't. It takes over your life, Ruth. And if you cut too deeply it might even take your life. Is that what you want?"

I actually feel tears coming now. I try to fight them, but it's like I'm going to burst. I press my palms against my eyes.

"Go ahead," she tells me. "Just cry. It's the first step toward healing."

And so, feeling like the dam has burst, I sit there and cry. Nicole hands me a box of tissues, and I must go through about a dozen before I stop. I can't remember the last time I cried that much. Or maybe I can. Maybe it was last winter. At Christmastime. Right after I found out that my mom tried to kill herself.

"Okay," says Nicole. "This is your journal assignment for today, Ruth. I want you to write about whatever it is you're thinking about right now. Can you do that?"

I nod. "Yeah, I think so."

"Why don't you stay here in my office and get started," she says. "And I'll go tell Juanita that she needs to check your stuff. And you can make it easier by just telling us where you've hidden it."

I unzip my backpack and remove my Altoids box, open it up, remove the paper, and show her the blade taped to the bottom.

"Clever," she says as she takes it. "I hadn't seen that trick yet. But then I can tell you're a smart girl, Ruth."

And as insignificant as that one little compliment might seem to a normal person, it means more than I can even begin to explain. I pull out my journal. Most of the entries so far haven't been more than a couple of sentences. Mostly I just try to avoid writing anything at all. But in the quiet privacy of Nicole's office, I begin to write about how I was actually feeling six months ago. Back when life as I knew it really started falling apart.

It's not like we were ever a "happy" family. I mean my dad had always been hard on us. Mom used to jokingly call him "Mr. Grisly Bear" when he was in a foul mood. And she would warn Caleb and me sometimes by quietly signaling that Dad was in one of his moods. And she was actually fairly good at "detonating" him sometimes. Occasionally she could even make him laugh at his own grumpiness.

But it seemed like it got harder and harder with each passing year. And I suppose that it didn't help things when Caleb and I became teenagers. I remember last year when I turned fifteen and wanted to get my learner's permit to drive. Naturally, I didn't ask my dad. I went straight to Mom. And, naturally, she had no problem with it. She thought it would be great for me to learn to drive. "You can run errands and pick up Caleb for me," she happily told me.

So I studied hard and she took me for the test, which I aced, but when Dad heard the news, he totally blew his top. He questioned Mom's sanity for allowing me to get my permit. He accused her of going behind his back and all sorts of things. Instead of being happy for me, he made me feel like a criminal. After that, Mom only took me driving a few times. I could tell it worried her a lot. Like she was afraid I'd get into a fender-bender and she'd be in hot water. Finally I just quit asking her to teach me to drive. It wasn't worth it.

I know that wasn't the real turning point, but it seemed like Mom went downhill pretty steadily after that. It's like something inside of her was dying. She hardly ever smiled anymore. And she seemed to be avoiding Dad, then us, then life in general.

I suppose we shouldn't have been all that shocked when she tried to kill herself. But at the time, I was totally stunned. I also thought that it was my fault. Because when I asked my dad, "Why? Why did she do it?" he said Caleb and I were driving her crazy. And then, when I started to cry, he told me to "grow up!" that "tears are for babies" and that "he wasn't going to put up with any more weakness."

After that, I hid my tears if I cried. And after a while, I learned to hold my tears in.

Sure, it hurt. But I guess I thought if I could contain it long enough, maybe it would eventually go away. Instead, the pain seemed to get worse. I felt like I should be wearing a sign that warned bystanders to stand back, that "contents were under pressure" and I could blow any moment . . .

On and on I write, losing track of the time. But the words just keep pouring out of me, like the pressure valve has finally been released. Not completely. That might be dangerous. But little by little, word by word, I can feel myself beginning to relax just a tiny bit.

"It's dinnertime," says a voice I don't recognize.

I look up to see a girl about my height with long brown hair. She's vaguely familiar, but I don't think I've actually met her, and she's not in my small group.

"I'm Cassie," she tells me. "I'm your new roommate."

"Oh." I feel a little guilty now. I still can't believe I was so mean to Alexi. I wonder if I should apologize or at least watch my backside.

"Don't worry," she says as if she knows what I'm thinking.

"You're not the first one to complain about sharing a room with Alexi. And she's the one who asked for a new roommate."

"Oh."

"Anyway, Nicole asked me to come and get you."

"Right." I close my journal and stash it in my backpack. "Thanks."

As I walk with Cassie toward the dining room, I feel a faint glimmer of hope. Of course, hope has fooled me before. And I'm sure I'll be fooled again. But this bit of hope actually feels like the real thing.

twenty

IT'S NOT LIKE EVERYTHING SUDDENLY GETS EASY AND GROOVY AND WONDERFUL for me at Promise House. I still have to endure a lot of hard work and frustration. Sometimes I just want to walk out of this place and never come back. And other times I'm looking around for a potentially sharp object like broken glass, a piece of metal, even a paperclip . . . and I imagine secretly cutting myself in an effort to dull the pain of really looking at my life and all its dark corners.

Sometimes I wonder if that strong pull, that irresistible urge to cut, will ever go away. Will I carry it with me for life? Like some of these scars?

Even so, I haven't given in for four whole days now. I think that's a personal record. However, if I'm to be perfectly honest with myself, the way that Nicole keeps saying we must be, I don't think I'm over this yet.

Still, it feels like I've turned a corner. And by the beginning of my second week, I'm sharing a little better during the group sessions. Even though it turns into a yelling match at times—often me against Alexi, who still seems to hate my guts—Nicole says I'm making progress.

I've even earned a few phone calls (one of our little rewards for good behavior) and I used them to call Abby and Glen and even

Uncle Rod. Abby had already guessed that I went someplace to deal with my cutting problem; she didn't say much about it and I didn't either—it was just easier that way. And no way could I work up the nerve to tell Glen or even my uncle the real truth. But I did assure Glen that my time away from home was making a difference. It's like I wanted him to think I was off on some sort of mental-health vacation. Fortunately, he didn't ask for any details but simply seemed happy for me. And I was relieved to find out, via Uncle Rod, that my mom has gone to live with Grandma Donna and Caleb. I can imagine how crowded it must be in that little mobile home, but I'm sure my mom's relieved to be there, to be away from my dad. I know I am.

Of course, I have no idea how my dad's taking all this. It must be so weird for him to be rambling around in his empty house with no one to yell at, no one to blame or accuse or belittle. I wonder if the place is getting really messy, since he never cleans up after himself. I have to admit that I like the idea of him digging through the dirty laundry hamper for a work shirt or a pair of matching socks. And I love the idea of the garbage piling up all over the garage and dirty dishes teetering on the counter. I really, really hope that he's suffering. I hope he realizes what he lost—or what he threw away.

It's getting easier to journal about these things now. In fact, I'm sure that I'll fill this notebook before long, and I might even need another. Writing about feelings really is good therapy. It's like a safe place to say the hard stuff. And no one needs to see it.

"Remember that it takes a good habit to replace a bad habit," Nicole is telling us today. Okay, I've heard this line from her before, but I think maybe it's actually beginning to sink in now. "The thing is," she says with emphasis, "even if you make the choice to completely quit cutting, that old impulse to cut will remain with you. Like any addiction, the *compulsion* can be as strong as the actual behavior.

You've got to find something to replace this urge—something that will help to devour the urge to hurt yourself."

Some of the newer girls seem confused by this. And I guess I know how they feel.

"Say that you've had a problem with rats," she continues. "They've infested your house, they're chewing on your furniture, eating your food, and pooping all over the place. So you decide you've had enough. You're fed up, so you set out some traps, maybe even live traps if you're opposed to killing anything. This is like making the decision to quit cutting. You're done with this thing for good. So you set your traps, and before long the rats are gone and life is cool. You relax and kick back, you throw the nasty traps away, and you're ready to enjoy life as normal. What's going to happen next?"

"The rats come back," says someone from the back. Someone who's obviously been here long enough to guess the answer.

"Right," she says. "Like your decision to quit cutting, the traps were a good start, but seriously—who wants a bunch of rat traps sitting around their house 24/7? They're not very pretty, and it's not much fun to keep removing the rats from the traps."

"Yeah, you're grossing me out," says someone.

"So, what if you found something more pleasant to keep the rats away? Like what if you got a nice, friendly cat? What happens then?"

"No more rats?" says someone else.

"Exactly. You replace the bad habit with a good one. Cats instead of rats. Something that helps to keep the bad habit from coming back. What can you use as your cat, Charisa? What do you do when you get the urge to cut? Something that helps you to move on and avoid going backward?"

"My guitar?" Charisa slouches, bored, like maybe she's been in this class too long too. Then she perks up a little. "And I just started writing songs," she adds. "I even wrote one about cutting."

"And it's really good," says her roommate, Jessica, the girl I thought was stupid because she started cutting when her dog died. But what I didn't know was that her parents had just divorced and then her grandmother was diagnosed with cancer. Turns out the dog was just the tip of her iceberg.

"That's great," says Nicole. "And what's your cat, Jessica? What habit are you replacing cutting with?"

"Knitting."

Charisa laughs. "And at the rate you're going, you'll have knitted a square mile before you get out of here." Everyone knows how Jessica is obsessed with knitting these little patches. They're about six inches square, and she keeps them in a plastic garbage bag. They are seriously starting to pile up.

"What are you going to do with them?" asks another girl.

"I don't know." She shrugs as if she doesn't really care.

"Maybe you should make a blanket," suggests my roommate, Cassie.

A few others talk about their replacement habits, their "cats." But I feel kind of stuck now. I realize I've been journaling a lot, and that helps. But that's something everyone does. It doesn't seem like a great replacement.

"How about you, Ruth?" Nicole finally asks me. "Have you thought of anything yet?"

"I don't know," I say. "I mean, other than journaling about how I feel, I'm not sure."

"What do you *love* to do?" asks Jessica suddenly.

I just shrug. The truth is, I'm not sure that I *love* doing anything. That kind of excitement is just foreign to me.

"You do like to draw," offers Cassie. "I've seen you making little doodles and sketches in your journal. And they're really good."

I nod. "Yeah, I actually do like art a lot. But I've never done much of anything with it outside of school." And then I start to connect the dots for myself. "But that was because of my dad," I confess. "I didn't want him to make fun of me. It hurt too much."

"I know just what you mean," says Charisa. "I'm exactly like that with my music too. I hate when someone in my family says something about it. It makes me want to smash my guitar . . . or, well, you know, cut . . . "

And suddenly we're all talking. We're worried about whether we'll be able to continue with our replacement habits once we go home. What if we fail? What if we fall back into the old patterns? But as we talk, we also manage to encourage each other, and some girls make suggestions for others. We talk about how we need to surround ourselves with friends who support and encourage us, people who understand that we need a replacement habit to keep the old one away.

Finally, we come up with the catchphrase "Don't kill the cat," which means, keep your replacement habit alive and well.

That evening I find a sketch pad and package of sketching pencils sitting on my bed, and I put them to good use doing a caricature of a grinning feline with a mouse under her paw. The caption is "Don't kill the cat." Cassie likes it so much that she shows it to Nicole, who, with my permission, makes photocopies of it for the other girls. And they actually ask me to autograph them, like I'm famous. Ha-ha. Although I admit, it feels pretty good.

By the end of the second week, I'm feeling stronger. Oh sure, the urge to cut is still there, but it's not constant now. The group therapy sessions can be aggravating at times. And sometimes they even feel fairly redundant. But just the same, I have to admit they're helping. I guess some things have to be pounded into you before you really believe it.

Sketching has become my main replacement habit—my cat. That and deep breathing. Also, Nicole teaches a class in yoga stretches and relaxation techniques, and I find myself actually using these at times too. Still, I'm not sure that all this is enough. I still get frightened, like, what if I go back to cutting again, or what if I'm incurable? I know there are no guarantees. Sometimes, like when I start worrying about my family and obsessing about what's going to happen to me when I get out of here, the temptation to cut is as strong as ever.

"Admitting you have a problem is the first step toward real healing," Nicole is saying for like the umpteenth time. And I think I've mostly gotten this. I mean, I do talk fairly openly about my problem now, and I don't pretend like I don't belong in Promise House anymore, and everyone here knows without a doubt that I'm a cutter. But I still feel like I'm holding back a little.

For one thing, I still keep my arms covered up. Partly because I'm ashamed, and partly because I don't want to see my ugly scars. I don't want to be reminded of my own stupidity. Other girls go around in tank tops, and some of their scars are way worse than mine. But it's like they're okay with it. Like they don't need to hide it anymore. I'm not there yet.

On my fifteenth day, I decide it's time to take another step. So I go to the health room and ask Juanita if I can borrow some scissors. She gives me a serious questioning look that seems to say, *Yeah, sure. I'm going to give a cutter a sharp object, you bet.*

"To cut the sleeves off some of my shirts," I explain. "All I brought with me were these long sleeves and I—"

"Oh, yes. Of course." She reaches into a drawer and hands me some scissors. "But only shirts, Ruth."

I kind of laugh, but to be perfectly honest, as I carry the stainless-steel scissors upstairs, I do wonder what it would feel like to cut again. Oh, I know I'm not really going to do it. Not right now anyway. But the truth is, I *wonder*. And it bugs me that I would feel this way, that my brain still insists on going back there, even after two weeks without it. Man, I wish I could wipe that part of my brain clean.

I use the scissors to make a couple shirts short-sleeved and several others entirely sleeveless. It's not much, but it's a start. Then I actually put on one of the sleeveless tops and go downstairs to return the scissors. "See," I tell Juanita, holding up my scarred but not bleeding arms.

"Good girl."

Okay, I have to admit this is really, really hard at first. I cannot stand to look at my arms. They make me feel sick inside—like I'm such a stupid loser. Oh sure, this is a good visual reminder of why I never want to go back to cutting. But the scars are so ugly. So freaking ugly. Sometimes I look down and see them, and I get really angry at myself for ever doing this in the first place. I get so angry that I actually want to hurt myself. But that's when I remember I can do something else. I can sketch. I can breathe. I can do a little yoga. Or, better yet, I can talk to someone.

It really helps having these other girls around me, girls who've been to the same dark places, girls who understand the pain. But I still wish more than anything that I'd never done it at all. And I still call myself "stupid" every time I see my scars.

"Shut off the internal bashing," Nicole warns us again and again. "You're all doing it," she says as she points her finger at our small group. "You call yourself names. You lay on guilt trips, you take the blame for everything." Then she points at me. "Right now, Ruth, what is the name you most often call yourself?"

"Stupid," I say without even thinking.

"Well, it's a lie!" she practically shouts. "What do you guys think? Is Ruth stupid?"

"Sometimes she is," says Alexi with a mean grin.

"She's smart," says Jessica.

"She's intelligent," says Cassie. "I bet her IQ is really high."

"See," says Nicole. "You are *not* stupid. That's just a label someone else gave you. It's not the truth. What are some of the other labels you girls have given yourselves?"

And so we go around some more. Girls confess what they tell themselves, their inner dialogue, and we in turn refute it. We tell them it's a lie, we tell them what we see as the truth.

"The Bible says, *You shall know the truth,*" Nicole eventually says, as she writes this sentence on the whiteboard: *"And the truth shall set you free."*

Okay, by now I know that Nicole is a Christian. But she doesn't shove her religion down anyone's throat. It's like it's just a part of who she is. For whatever reason, it works for her. My roommate, Cassie, is also a Christian. And although I really like her and she's a sweet and caring person, I do get a little tired of her trying to "save me."

"I don't need that," I've told her over and over. "I mean, it's fine for you and Nicole and some of the other girls. But I personally don't need it. Okay?"

"How can you *not* need God?" she persists. "Everyone needs God. Maybe you just don't understand that yet. But you will, Ruth. Someday you will."

"Maybe someday. But not today. Okay?" I usually turn back to my sketch, hoping she'll take the hint.

"Well, I'm going to keep praying for you," she says, like it's a big warning.

"Whatever trips your trigger," I toss back.

But here's the truth: I am beginning to wonder if the Christians might be onto something. It's like I can see this difference between the girls who are taking God seriously and the ones like me, who are not. And it's the ones who are taking God seriously, like Cassie, who seem to be making better progress. It's like they have some kind of inner strength that the rest of us are missing. I wish I was imagining this whole thing, but I'm afraid I am not.

To be perfectly honest, I'm not really sure what my problem with God is. It's possible that since I've heard God called "the Father" that I'm thinking he may be just like my dad. And that's pretty freaky. I mean, what if he's angry at me too? I just cannot deal with any more anger or disapproval, especially from someone as big as God. I don't need it.

And yet I find myself thinking about God a lot, and I'm wondering if Cassie is right. Maybe I am missing something. I suppose this all has something to do with the The Cutter's Twelve Steps, a paper that Nicole gave each of us to read and study daily.

I've read these steps once a day since I've been here. But I have to admit that I feel slightly stumped when I come to the steps that include "a Higher Power." Unfortunately, most of the Twelve Steps are based on this.

The Cutter's Twelve Steps to Recovery

1. We admit we are powerless over our illness of self-mutilation and cutting.
2. We believe that a Higher Power can restore us to wellness.

3. We make a choice to turn our will and our lives over to the care of our Higher Power, to help us to rebuild our lives in a positive and caring way.

4. We make an honest and fearless personal inventory of ourselves.

5. We admit to our Higher Power, to ourselves, and to others, the exact nature of our weaknesses and our strengths.

6. We are willing to have our Higher Power remove all our weaknesses.

7. We humbly ask our Higher Power to remove our weaknesses and to strengthen and heal us.

8. We make a list of anyone we have hurt by hurting ourselves, and we make a plan to make amends.

9. We make direct amends to such people wherever possible, except when to do so would injure them or others or ourselves.

10. We continue to take personal inventory, and when we blow it, we admit it, while we continue to recognize our progress.

11. We seek, through prayer and meditation, to improve our conscious contact with our Higher Power, praying to know our Higher Power's will for us and for the power to carry it out.

12. When we have experienced a spiritual awakening as a result of these steps, we carry this message to others who cut or mutilate and commit ourselves to a life of wholeness and healing.

"I personally don't think anyone can successfully stop cutting on her own," Nicole has told us on a regular basis. "At least I don't know of anyone who has. I really believe that you need a supernatural kind of help. Something beyond what you can pull out of yourself. So don't be afraid to ask *God* for help. He's ready to give it."

So, once more I am reading the Twelve Steps. And I realize I haven't really made it much further than the first step. That's probably because the very next step involves this Higher Power thing. So I'm trying to become more open to it. For the first time in my life, I am trying to take God more seriously. I just hope that he's not mad at me for messing up so badly in the first place.

twenty-one

BY THE END OF MY THIRD WEEK, I FEEL STUCK. LIKE I CAN'T GO FORWARD AND I don't want to go back. I schedule a private counseling session with Nicole for Friday afternoon.

"What's up, Ruth?" She leans back in the chair behind her desk.

"I'm stuck."

She sits up straight now. "What do you mean, stuck?"

"I think it has to do with the Twelve Steps," I tell her. "I can do some of them, but I get stuck on the others."

She nods like she knows what I mean. "The ones that involve a Higher Power?"

"Yeah."

"Do you believe in God, Ruth?"

"Yeah. I guess I do."

"Do you have a relationship with him?"

"A *relationship*?"

"Like, do you talk to him? Do you pray?"

I shake my head. "My family used to go to church when I was little. Mostly because my mom wanted to. Then we stopped. I guess I just never gave God much thought."

"What do you think God thinks of you?"

I shrug. "Not much, I guess."

"That's where you're wrong, Ruth. God loves you. I mean he totally loves you. So much that he poured himself into a human being—his Son, Jesus—and actually died for you."

"I know a little about Jesus," I tell her. "I've heard how he died on a cross, but I have to admit that I don't really get that. I mean, it seems so archaic and brutal, so barbaric. Like something that happened when people were less civilized and lived so differently from now. You know. Like it's not really relevant today."

She kind of smiles now. "Like physical pain and suffering isn't relevant, Ruth?"

I'm not sure what she means and so I just wait.

"Why did you cut yourself?"

I'm wondering if this is a trick question now. But all I can do is tell the truth. "To make the pain go away."

"Did it?"

"For a while . . . you know how it is."

"But do you wonder why you had this need to hurt yourself, to make yourself bleed, to inflict pain and suffering?"

I nod. "Yeah, I guess I sort of do."

"Does it seem barbaric, archaic, brutal?"

Suddenly it's like this tiny light comes on, and I actually feel goose bumps on my arms, right on top of the scars. "What exactly do you mean?"

"You've seen the poster that's in all the bedrooms," she says to me. "'By his stripes you are healed.' Do you know what that means?"

I shake my head.

"It's from the Bible," she says. "It's referring to Jesus' stripes. He was whipped thirty-nine times across the back. Enough to kill a man. He was bloody and beaten. And that was only the beginning."

"But what does it mean?"

"It means that God understands our struggles. He understands that it would *take pain to remove pain*. But he also understands that we can't do it ourselves. And so he stepped in—he came to earth in the form of Jesus Christ—and he took that pain, that beating, that death upon himself so you and I don't have to, Ruth. We don't need to cut ourselves or make ourselves bleed to get rid of the pain. Jesus did it for us. He allowed himself to be beaten and killed—like you said, brutally and barbarically—so that we could escape the pain."

I actually feel tears in my eyes now. I'm not even sure why, but somehow I get what Nicole is saying. Okay, maybe my head doesn't quite grasp it yet, but something deeper does.

"Do you know what that means, Ruth?"

"Sort of."

"It means that God let Jesus take our pain, he let him bleed and die, and then he raised him from the dead, so that we can be made whole. So that we can have a relationship with God, *the* Higher Power, *the* Ruler of the Universe. By Jesus' stripes we are healed. Do you understand now?"

Tears are coming down my cheeks now. "Yeah, I think I do." And then Nicole asks me if I want to pray with her, if I want to become whole by inviting Jesus into my heart. And I do. So we pray this very simple and straightforward prayer, and she says, "Amen." And that's it.

Then she hugs me and gives me a couple of books. "This one's just some basics about being a Christian," she says. "And this is the New Testament."

"Is that like the Bible?" I feel pretty dumb.

"Yeah. It's the Jesus part of the Bible."

And since I have about an hour before dinnertime, I take these up to my room and sit down and start reading the New Testament. I decide to start right at the beginning, like maybe I have some catching up to do.

"What're you reading?" asks Cassie when she comes in just before six.

I hold up the New Testament and her eyes light up. "No way!" She comes over to get a better look.

So I tell her about my conversation with Nicole and how I prayed, and she throws her arms around me and starts crying. "That is so cool, that is so cool," she says again and again.

And I have to agree with her. It is pretty cool. And now I feel like things are changing in me, not just surface things, but deep things, from the inside out. And the next time I read through the Twelve Steps, they begin to make more sense. And suddenly I don't feel stuck at all.

For the first time, I go to Nicole's Bible-study session on Sunday morning. It's completely voluntary and something I had absolutely no interest in attending before. Today I can't wait. I've already read the first four books of the Bible and am full of questions and thoughts. Cassie and I go down to the meeting room together, and I'm surprised that there are only a handful of girls there. But, like me, each of them has a Bible and a notebook, and they seem eager to be there. And after Nicole asks Cassie to pray for our time together, she begins.

"Today we're going to learn about forgiveness," she announces. Then she has us all look up Bible verses. Cassie helps me to find mine.

Nicole breaks forgiveness down into three categories, writing them on the whiteboard. We need to be forgiven by God; we need to forgive others; we need to forgive ourselves. Then she explains how this works. The first one comes fairly easy to me. I do see the need to be forgiven by God. I mean, I do not want him to be mad at me or hold anything against me. But she, and the Bible verses, assure us that God is all about love and forgiveness, and I am coming to the place where I can accept that God is *nothing* like my dad.

The second part about forgiving is a little tougher for me. I mean, I can forgive my mom, since a lot of what happened isn't really her fault. And I can forgive Caleb for running out because I understand that he was really frustrated. And I might even be able to forgive my grandparents for letting me down. But I don't think I'll ever be able to forgive my dad. Why should I even want to? The guy is a total jerk. But I don't say this out loud.

The third step is about forgiving myself. And while I'd like to be able to do this, I can tell it's going to be tough.

"This is the deal," Nicole finally says. "No one can do this all at once. And no one can do this without God's help. He's the expert on forgiving, and he's the only one who can give you what you need to forgive—either yourself or others. So all you need to do is go to him and tell him that you need his help. Pretty simple, huh?"

We all kind of nod. But I suspect we may have similar questions, similar challenges.

"But simple's not always easy," she continues. "Just know that God is prepared to equip us for everything he asks us to do. So go to him first."

Well, that's a little comforting. This whole thing is so new to me and a bit overwhelming. But if all I need to do is go to him first, it doesn't seem too complicated. And so that's what I decide to do. I take a walk out on the grounds and talk to God. I ask him to help me with this whole forgiveness thing. And then I get a real sense of peace. Like I know God has forgiven me, and I get the feeling he's going to help me to forgive myself and others too. Maybe it won't happen all at once, but I get the feeling it will happen.

And I'm thinking I can trust him with that.

twenty-two

DURING MY FOURTH AND FINAL WEEK AT PROMISE HOUSE, NICOLE TELLS ME that it's time to write my "emancipation letter."

"What's that?" I ask. "My ticket out of here?"

"Not exactly. It's more like your ticket back to where you came from."

"Oh." Now this is not a happy thought. And I'm sure my face is showing it.

"I don't mean going back to the same old problems, Ruth. You're not the same person you were when you came here, and you will not return to the same old mess. But one of the things we want girls to do before they go back is to write a letter that will help to free them from returning to the destructive lifestyle. That's why it's called an emancipation letter."

"Oh." Still, I'm not quite getting it. "Who do I write it to?"

"You kind of write it to yourself. But then you send it to whoever is part of your life. Usually you send it to parents and siblings, any extended family that you're close to, and to good friends and boyfriends when applicable. Mainly the people, good or bad, who've been pretty involved in your life."

"Oh."

"I've got a couple of samples here, if that would help." She hands me a few sheets of paper. "In a way, they sound kind of like the Twelve Steps, only more personal. It's like your chance to proclaim that you've had a problem, but are getting well now. And it's a way to let people know that you need support. Also, you can let people who are a negative influence know that you've changed, you won't play by their rules anymore. You know?"

I nod. "Yeah, I sort of get it." And so I take the sample letters to my room to read them and then sit and think about what I'd like to write.

After several bad beginnings, it starts coming to me. I eventually make a fairly good draft. Okay, I'll admit it sounds a little formal at first, but maybe that's the best way to get this across. Then I go over the draft again, make a few changes, and finally I rewrite the whole thing in my best handwriting. I think I've pretty much nailed it.

To Whom It May Concern:

I, Ruth Anne Wallace, admit to being a cutter. A cutter is a person who self-mutilates her body (in my case with a razor blade on my arms) in order to escape the pain in her life. Unfortunately, cutting, an addictive behavior, does not solve your problems. In fact, it only makes them worse. That's why I'm being treated at Promise House, and because of that treatment, I am now ready to face life without giving in to this destructive behavior.

Some of you may wonder why I felt the need to cut. I wondered this myself. The pain I was trying to escape came directly from my dad's constant verbal abuse. I've lived with it most of my life, but it got worse after my mom had her breakdown. I believe her breakdown was the direct result of my dad's constant verbal attacks on her. She was miserable and tried to take her own life. Losing my mom's support was what finally pushed me over the edge to cutting.

I believe this is also the reason my brother Caleb ran away from home. He couldn't take it anymore. I don't know what will happen to me when I am released from Promise House, but I do know that I will no longer put up with my dad's verbal abuse. If I have to get a job and support myself, I will. But I refuse to go back to the toxic environment that I grew up in.

I also want to say that while at Promise House, I became a Christian, and I believe that God is going to help me to get through this. And I'm sorry for anyone that I've hurt when I was hurting myself.

Sincerely,

Ruth Anne Wallace

I turn my emancipation letter in to Nicole Tuesday afternoon, and Wednesday morning she gives me twelve stamped envelopes and twelve copies of my letter. "Good job, Ruth," she says. "Let me know if you need more copies or envelopes."

"I'm sure this is way more than enough," I tell her.

"There are phone books for most cities in the state in the office," she tells me. "In case you need to look up some addresses."

So I sit down and carefully address the envelopes. And I'm surprised that I use all twelve copies of my letter, keeping the original for myself. Here is my list:

Mom
Caleb

Grandma Donna
Uncle Rod
Grandma and Grandpa Wallace
Uncle Garrett
Abby
Glen
Ms. Blanchard
Mr. Pollinni
Dad

And I put my name on the last one, without an address, and I slip it into the back of my notebook.

I feel a little worried as I take my eleven sealed envelopes downstairs to put in the mail. I mean, no one on my list, besides Abby and Ms. Blanchard, has any idea about what's going on with me. I've been tempted to tell Glen during our weekly phone calls, and I suppose I've even dropped some hints. But he's been so great about me being gone, and he seems so into me, that I just couldn't bear to risk everything. Until now. But, I tell myself, what choice do I have? I can't hide this thing forever. Either he'll be able to handle it or not. Time will tell.

But instead of obsessing and freaking, I do remember to ask God to take care of these things. Then I hand over my letters to Juanita, and as I walk away, I feel an amazing new sense of freedom, like I've just come clean with everyone and I no longer have anything to hide. In a way, it's exhilarating. I have no idea how anyone will react. Especially Glen. But in some ways I don't even care. It's like I really am free!

It's only as I come to the end of my final week that I begin to fully realize my time here will be finished on Sunday. Then I start to get concerned. What happens next? And am I really ready to go back home and face my dad?

I confess these fears during my last group session on Friday. "I'm starting to freak," I tell my friends (some who are new, a few who came here about the same time that I did). "I'm afraid that I might fall apart. I might end up like I was before, or even worse."

They remind me that I'm stronger now, that I have skills to use, and that I've changed.

"You're so strong, Ruth," says a new girl named Katy. She's only fourteen and has only been cutting for a couple of months. "I mean, I really look up to you as kind of a role model here. You always have such good things to say during our small group. I know you're going to do great when you go back."

I wish I had Katy's kind of confidence in myself. While it's encouraging and I hope that she's right, I'm still not sure that I'm as strong as she thinks.

"This is one of those times when you really have to trust in your Higher Power," says Nicole. "You need to remember that you *cannot* do this on your own. You *do* need help. Just ask for it. God will show up, Ruth. Just trust him and see what he can do."

So I'm trying to do that. And every time I start to freak, I remind myself that it's time to pray—it's time to ask God for help. And by Sunday morning, I am amazingly relaxed.

After Bible study is finished, I talk to Nicole privately. First, I thank her for everything she's done for me, and then I promise to stay in touch.

"But what's next?" I ask. "I mean, I know that today's my last day. But when do I leave? And how do I get home?" The last time I asked her about this, she said to wait and see. "I guess I could go stand out on the road and hold out my thumb."

She laughs. "Yeah, we usually make our girls hitch a ride home when they're done here."

"But seriously, am I going home today?"

"That's what we told you, isn't it? Are you packed and ready?"

"Yeah." I frown now. "But the suspense is killing me. And, please, please, don't tell me my dad is picking me up."

She shakes her head. "I already promised you that would not happen. And the only reason I didn't tell you anything more was because I wasn't sure myself."

"You're not sure?"

"Well, I am now. My sister is coming to get you. And she has some things to talk to you about. She should be here just after lunch. Can you wait that long?"

I smile. "No problem."

I use my last couple of hours to say good-bye to the girls and to take one last walk around the grounds. And during this walk I, once again, ask for God's help. I feel like such a beginner right now. Like I have so much to learn—about God, about myself, and others. But I feel like this time I'm going to do things right. And this time will be different from the others, because God is going to help me get through this.

I sit down on a sunny bench, my favorite thinking spot, and look down at my arms. The scars have faded a lot. Especially after I started using Juanita's "secret formula," which is a lotion she concocts of aloe vera and coconut oil. And this mixture seems to help as I get a little tan on my arms, making the scars fade instead of standing out. Even so, I have a feeling that some of the scars will be with me always. Maybe they'll be a good reminder. A reminder of two things: (1) I don't need to hurt myself anymore, and (2) by his stripes (not mine) I am healed.

twenty-three

MS. BLANCHARD PICKS ME UP AT ONE THIRTY, AND AFTER DOZENS OF HUGS AND several sweet gifts, including a patchwork scarf knitted by Jessica (she eventually put her squares together to make lots of scarves for all her Promise House friends), we are on our way.

"You look wonderful," Ms. Blanchard tells me as she heads for the highway.

"Thanks. I feel great too." Then I thank her for all she did to help get me into Promise House.

"I'm so glad I could help," she says. "My heart just went out to you the first time I saw you sitting outside my office. Of course, I'd read a bit of your file, enough to know your family was having some problems, and that you were a good student. Anyway, I think God just tugged on my heart and I couldn't let you slip through some crack before school got out."

I take a deep breath now, then slowly exhale. "Nicole said you have some things to tell me. But mostly I want to know where you are taking me. Do I have to go back to my dad now?"

"I won't lie to you, Ruth. It's been tricky. As you know, your mom's a little better, but she's still got a long way to go. And it's pretty crowded where they're living, but we did get Children's Protective Services to agree to give Donna temporary custody of Caleb. It'll be reviewed again before school starts."

"Well, that's good. I mean, that it's okay for him to be there for now."

"Yes. But I had some problems convincing Protective Services that it wasn't in your best interest to be returned to your previous home. Without anything on file against your dad—no police reports or prior convictions—well, it just wasn't going too well."

"Oh." I feel my heart sinking now, a giant lump growing in my throat. I silently pray.

"But then your letter from Promise House came." She turns and smiles at me now. "And that changed some things."

"Really?"

"Well, your Grandma Wallace really stepped up to the plate. She arranged a family meeting with your dad and his brother, and they all sat down and had a big talk. And, somehow, it was decided that you should come live with your grandparents. At least for the summer. Will that work for you?"

I'm nodding now. "Yeah. That would be great."

"And that gives everyone time to figure things out. According to your other grandma, your mom's mom, they would like to work something out to get you and Caleb and your mom back together. Your mom's goal is to get well enough to go back to work and possibly support you kids."

"Really?"

"Yes. But it's still a way out. In the meantime, it looks like you'll be in good hands at your grandparents' home."

I feel a small wave of relief washing over me now. I know everything's not completely settled, and I still have some major obstacles to face, including my dad. But I think I can handle it. With God, I can handle it.

As we get closer to town, I start feeling nervous again. I'm wondering what this is going to be like. I mean, having people know what I did, that I was a cutter. Will they look down on me? Will they pity me? What will it be like?

I forced myself to wear a sleeveless shirt today. Partly because it's like ninety degrees, and partly because I knew it would force me not to hide my scars. Now I'm not so sure that was the most brilliant idea. I look down at my arms, at my stripes . . . and then I remind myself that by *his* stripes I am healed.

As we turn down the street, I notice several cars parked at my grandparents' and suddenly get worried. What if something's wrong? What if they changed their minds? What if my dad's there? But I don't see his pickup. As we get closer, I see that some of the cars are familiar, and I see that some people are standing out in the front yard. And I see a banner kind of sign that says "Welcome Home, Ruth!"

Mom and Caleb are there. I hug them first. Then I see Abby and Glen and even Finney and a few other friends from school. And they hug me too. And while I notice some of my friends glancing down at my arms, uncomfortable at first, they quickly return to their same old selves. Then I hug my grandparents and thank them for letting me stay here, at least for now. I don't ask anyone about my dad. I'm not ready for that yet.

After I've had a chance to reacquaint myself with everyone, Glen takes me off to a quiet corner of my grandma's backyard. "You could've told me, Ruth," he says with a slightly hurt tone. "I would've understood."

I study his face and his sincerity slightly stuns me. "*Really?*"

He nods. "I kind of thought there was something going on with you, I mean, besides your dad. But I just wasn't sure what . . . "

"I'm sorry," I tell him. "It's just that I was really ashamed of . . . well, the whole cutting thing." I held out my arms as part of my confession. "I was afraid you'd think I was crazy."

He smiles then pulls me into a tight hug. "Hey, we're all a little crazy."

By the end of the day, I feel tired but good. I imagine it's the way you'd feel after climbing a mountain. Even better than that, I feel peaceful. There's a new calmness inside me that still takes me by surprise. Oh, I'm not stupid. I know that it's something that needs to be maintained. I fully realize that this peace, this calm, this serenity is a result of me staying connected to God. And just as my commitment *not* to cut will remain a daily thing, so will my commitment to him. One day at a time. I think I can handle that.

reader's guide

1. How did you feel when you read the first scene where Ruth cut herself? Were you repulsed, confused, intrigued? Explain your feelings.

2. Ruth began cutting shortly after her mom's breakdown. How might she have handled things differently?

3. Abby was the first one to discover Ruth's "dirty little secret." How do you think it made Abby feel?

4. How do you think Abby could've been more helpful to Ruth? What would you do if you had a friend who was a cutter?

5. Have you ever done, or considered doing, any form of self-harm? Explain.

6. Nicole explains that cutting is an addictive behavior. Do you have any addictive behaviors? Describe them.

7. Remember how Ruth journaled about bottling her pain? How do you deal with emotional pain in your own life?

8. If you met Ruth while she was still actively cutting, what would you have said to her?

9. Do you think Ruth will ever be able to forgive her dad? Why or why not?

10. What does "by his stripes you are healed" mean to you personally?

TrueColors Book 8

Bitter Rose

Coming in January 2006

*How was she supposed to hold her life together
when her family was breaking apart?*

One

LIFE AS I KNEW IT ENDED TODAY. SERIOUSLY, IT'S OVER. NOW YOU MAY THINK I'm just being a drama queen, and it wouldn't be the first time I've been accused of blowing something way out of proportion. But, trust me, this is the real deal. It's over.

"What's wrong?" asks my best friend, Claire, when she finally returns my call like two hours later.

"Everything," I tell her. "My life is over."

"What are you talking about, Maggie?"

"It's my parents."

"Are they fighting again?" Her voice sounds bored now, and slightly disconnected too, like I can just imagine her filing her nails, or maybe she's watching her favorite Home Shopping Network show, or reading her e-mail, or playing a stupid computer game.

"*Claire, this is serious.*"

"Oh, Maggie, your parents are constantly fighting. It'll blow over in—"

"No, it's *not* a fight this time. It's over! They are splitting up!"

"*Splitting up?*" She sounds a little shocked.

Okay, maybe I've got her attention now. "Yes! My mom just told me. Dad has left."

"No way!"

"Way."

"When did this happen?"

"Last night, apparently. I mean, there I was, going to youth group and spending the night at your house, just so they could have some one-on-one time, as my mom put it, and I come home today to discover that it's over. Dad's gone."

"What happened?"

"I'm not really sure. All Mom would tell me is that he's left and he's not coming back—" I start choking up now. I cannot believe my dad stepped out of my life just like that. I mean, he didn't even have the courtesy to warn me.

"Oh, Maggie, that's too bad. You were one of the few kids I know who still had her *original* parents. They actually gave me hope that love might possibly last forever."

"Apparently not."

"So where did your dad go anyway?"

"He's crashing with a friend for now. But Mom said he's going to get a place of his own soon."

"Did she say why? Like what actually brought it to this? Besides the fighting I mean?"

"No, she wouldn't say hardly anything about it. Then we just got into this huge old fight. I mean, it's clearly all her fault, Claire.

She's driven him away with her constant nagging and complaining. Who could stand to live with that woman? I know I can't! I walked out on her too."

"So where are you right now?"

"I'm sitting in my car."

"Where?"

"Outside of the mall. I know it's lame, but I didn't know where else to go."

"Well, come over here. Nobody's home but me anyway."

"Thanks, Claire." We say good-bye and I turn off my cell phone, worried that Mom might try to call again. She tried twice while I was waiting for Claire. Fortunately, I have my caller ID and I never picked up. But she did leave a message—a really pathetic one if you ask me.

"Hi, Magdela," she says in this depressed sounding voice. "I'm so sorry we fought. We really need to talk about this. Please, give me a call. I'm worried about you."

Well, she *should* be worried. It's because of her that my life is getting blown totally apart right now. And it's the beginning of my senior year, too—my last year at home, and the year when you really want the love and support of *both* your parents. My older brother and sister both got that much, but now they're off living their own lives and probably totally oblivious to the fact that our family is disintegrating—like, presto-chango, *poof!* it is gone.

And here's what really gets me—my parents, the respectable Roberto and Rosa Fernandez, are these born-again Catholic Christians, and they're all involved in their church and Bible study groups, and now *this*? I just don't get it. And they've always told us kids that marriage was a "forever commitment," that wedding vows were meant to be kept until "death do you part." So what's the deal here? Are they just total hypocrites or what? It's even making me question my own faith. I mean, if this is where it gets you—sheesh, why bother?

Finally, I'm at Claire's house. She meets me at the door with a big hug. "I'm so sorry, Maggie. I mean, speaking from experience, I know you'll survive, you'll get through this. But I know that it totally sucks too."

"You got that right."

As I follow her to the kitchen, I remind myself that Claire's parents got divorced when she was only ten. At the time, I was completely shocked and I felt so sorry for her and her mom. But time passed, and Jeannie eventually remarried a really nice guy, and I guess I just sort of forget about Claire's real dad. I think she sort of forgot him too, since he pretty much vanished out of her life. We never even talk about him anymore. But thinking of this doesn't make me feel a bit better. The truth is, I really love my dad. I mean he's not perfect, but he's pretty cool for a parent. And I don't want him to just disappear.

"You know what," I tell Claire as we dig our spoons into a half-full carton of cookie-dough ice cream. "I think I'll live with my dad."

Her eyebrows lift slightly. "Have you talked to him about this?"

"Of course not. I haven't even seen him since he left. But I'm sure he'll agree with me. I mean we've always gotten along a whole lot better than Mom and me. And lately, well, Mom's been pretty witchy to both of us. She's like this devil woman, always on everyone's case, always mad about something. She probably told him to leave. I just don't get it. Why did she do it? Why is she so horrible?" And now I burst into tears all over again. I will never forgive her for this!

about the author

MELODY CARLSON has written dozens of books for all age groups, but she particularly enjoys writing for teens. Perhaps this is because her own teen years remain so vivid in her memory. After claiming to be an atheist at the ripe old age of twelve, she later surrendered her heart to Jesus and has been following him ever since. Her hope and prayer for all her readers is that each one would be touched by God in a special way through her stories. For more information, please visit Melody's website at www.melodycarlson.com.

Diary of a Teenage Girl Series

Chloe

Diaries Are a Girl's Best Friend

MY NAME IS CHLOE, Chloe book one

Chloe Miller, Josh's younger sister, is a free spirit with dramatic clothes and hair. She struggles with her identity, classmates, parents, boys, and whether or not God is for real. But this unconventional high school freshman definitely doesn't hold back when she meets Him in a big, personal way. Chloe expresses God's love and grace through the girl band, Redemption, that she forms, and continues to show the world she's not willing to conform to anyone else's image of who or what she should be. Except God's, that is.
ISBN 1-59052-018-1

SOLD OUT, Chloe book two

Chloe and her fellow band members must sort out their lives as they become a hit in the local community. And after a talent scout from Nashville discovers the trio, all too soon their explosive musical ministry begins to encounter conflicts with family, so-called friends, and school. Exhilarated yet frustrated, Chloe puts her dream in God's hand and prays for Him to work out the details.
ISBN 1-59052-141-2

ROAD TRIP, Chloe book three

After signing with a major record company, Redemption's dreams are coming true. Chloe, Allie, and Laura begin their concert tour with the good-looking guys in the band Iron Cross. But as soon as the glitz and glamour wear off, the girls find life on the road a little overwhelming. Even rock-solid Laura appears to be feeling the stress—and Chloe isn't quite sure how to confront her about the growing signs of drug addiction...
ISBN 1-59052-142-0

FACE THE MUSIC, Chloe book four

Redemption has made it to the bestseller chart, but what Chloe and the girls need most is some downtime to sift through the usual high school stress with grades, friends, guys, and the prom. Chloe struggles to recover from a serious crush on the band leader of Iron Cross. Then just as an unexpected romance catches Redemption by surprise, Caitlin O'Conner—whose relationship with Josh is taking on a new dimension—joins the tour as a chaperone. Chloe's wild ride only speeds up, and this one-of-a-kind musician faces the fact that life may never be normal again.
ISBN 1-59052-241-9

Log onto www.DOATG.com

ALSO FROM MELODY CARLSON

Dark Blue: Color Me Lonely

Brutally ditched by her best friend, Kara feels totally abandoned until she discovers these dark blue days contain a life-changing secret.

1-57683-529-4

Deep Green: Color Me Jealous

Stuck in a twisted love triangle, Jordan feels absolutely green with envy until her former best friend, Kara, introduces her to someone even more important than Timothy.

1-57683-530-8

Torch Red: Color Me Torn

Zoë feels like the only virgin on the planet. But now that she's dating Justin Clark, it seems like that's about to change. Luckily, Zoë's friend Nate is there to try to save her from the biggest mistake of her life.

1-57683-531-6

Look for the TRUECOLORS series at a Christian bookstore near you or order online at www.navpress.com.

truecolors

THINK

ALSO FROM MELODY CARLSON

Pitch Black: Color Me Lost

Morgan Bergstrom thinks her life is as bad as it can get, but it's about to get a whole lot worse. Her close friend Jason Harding has just killed himself, and no one knows why. As she struggles with her grief, Morgan must make her life's ultimate decision — before it's too late.

1-57683-532-4

Burnt Orange: Color Me Wasted

Amber Conrad has a problem. Her youth group friends Simi and Lisa won't get off her case about the drinking parties she's been going to. *Everyone does it. What's the big deal?* Will she be honest with herself and her friends before things really get out of control?

1-57683-533-2

Fool's Gold: Color Me Consumed

On furlough from Papua New Guinea, Hannah Johnson spends some time with her Prada-wearing cousin Vanessa. Hannah feels like an alien around her host—everything Vanessa has is so nice. Hannah knows that stuff's not supposed to matter, but why does she feel a twinge of jealousy deep down inside?

1-57683-534-0

Look for the TrueColors series at a Christian bookstore near you or order online at www.navpress.com.

truecolors

THINK